FATAL FAREWELLS

A HISTORY OF UNUSUAL DEATHS

VOLUME II

Dear Matt,

Thank you so much once again, you are truly amazing!

Kind regards,
Matty Climpson

© 2025 by Matthew Climpson. All rights reserved.

For Evie & Isla

UPHOLDING THE LAW
CHARONDAS
6th CENTURY BCE

Charondas was a highly respected lawgiver from the port city of Catania, Sicily, sometime during the 6th century BCE. Historians are uncertain of exactly when he lived; some consider him to be a pupil of the ancient Ionian Greek philosopher Pythagoras (c. 580 - 504 BCE), but all that is known for certain is that Charondas lived earlier than Anaxilas of Rhegium, as the Rhegians abided by his laws until Anaxilas abolished them during the early years of the 5th century BCE. The legendary philosopher Plato spoke very positively about Charondas in his influential Socratic dialogue *The Republic,* while Aristotle's book entitled *Politics* heaped praise on him for the precise nature of his laws, especially those regarding homicide. Charondas' law also introduced penalties for committing perjury in court, the first instance of such laws being implemented in Sicily. Though his laws were not considered to be as harsh as those created by Draco of Athens, they were still quite brutal by the standards of that period in history. For example, deserters would be subjected to humiliation as they were put on display dressed in female clothing for the public to observe and ridicule them. Furthermore, those who refused to partake in jury duty service were given significant fines and had their reputations tarnished. These laws were based on the primitive concept of democracy at that time, with the majority of the population excluded from voting: slaves, women, minors, and certain types of business people. Original copies of these laws no longer exist; we only know of them through various reliable sources. Charondas wasn't exempt from his own regulations however - he would die breaking a law that he had created. According to the ancient Greek historian Diodorus Siculus, the lawgiver from Sicily had issued a strict law that anybody guilty of bringing weapons into the assembly in Catania must be executed, regardless of their importance. Charondas allegedly arrived at the assembly on an unspecified date to seek help in defeating a group of intruding brigands that had taken refuge in the nearby countryside. The lawgiver had absentmindedly forgotten to surrender his weapon before entering the building though, as he still had a sword attached to his belt, violating his own law. When it was pointed out to him that he was still in possession of a deadly weapon on forbidden ground, Charondas cried out in agreement and expressed disgust at making such a basic yet costly mistake. His recognition that he had broken the sacred laws of Catania left him with only one choice: to voluntarily take his own life. Charondas grabbed the large sword from his belt without hesitation and plunged it into his torso multiple times, killing himself - truly a man of principle. That single act of self-sacrifice proved that nobody is above the law, an important value that is still largely present in modern day society.

History of Greece: From the Earliest Times to the End of the Persian War - Volume 2, **PP. 334-337. Max Duncker (1886)**

The History of Sicily from the Earliest Times - Volume 2, **PP. 62-63. Edward Augustus Freeman (1891)**

Early Greek Law, **P. 66. Michael Gagarin (1989)**

The Origins of Radical Criminology: From Homer to Pre-Socratic Philosophy, **P. 16. Stratos Georgoulas (2018)**

https://www.ancient-origins.net/history/weapons-control-ancient-greece-accident-deadly-009735

IT ALL WENT PEAR-SHAPED

ANTIPHANES

c. 408 - 334 BCE

Antiphanes is often considered to be one of the most important writers of Middle Attic comedy. He was apparently a foreigner who settled in Athens, where he began to write about 387 BCE. The comic poet was extremely prolific: It's said he wrote over 300 comedies, and approximately 150 titles of the plays he wrote are known and various pieces of them have been preserved in Athenaeus. A large quantity of his plays highlighted matters that are connected to mythological subjects, while his other works mainly focused on the ethical principles and values of personal life. He was also a pioneer of the New Comedy - a form of Greek drama - during the later stages of his career. Very little is known about the playwright's life aside from his written work, and only small fragments of his writings have survived the test of time. However, the *Suda* - a lengthy 10th-Century Byzantine encyclopedia that contains vital information about the ancient Mediterranean world - provides a fascinating yet odd account of how Antiphanes died in 334 BCE. He was supposedly lingering under some fruit trees on the Greek island of Chios when a large pear fell from a tree branch and struck him on the top of his skull. Antiphanes died aged seventy-four from the blow to his head, which had likely fractured his skull and caused a severe hemorrhage. Arrangements were made to return his body to Athens - the site of his literary achievements - so he could receive an honorary burial.

A History of Greek Literature: from the Earliest Period to the Death of Demosthenes, **PP. 288-89. Frank Byron Jevons (1886)**

The Fragments of Attic Comedy Volume II, **P. 165. August Meineke, Theodor Bergk & Theodor Kock (1959)**

"Antiphanes". **Kenneth James Dover, Oxford Classical Dictionary (2012)**

The Eagle Times, 31st October 2023. "In Honor of Halloween, Centuries of Freaky Fatalities"

A VIOLENT DEMISE
OLD CROGHAN MAN
362 - 175 BCE

"Old Croghan Man" is a well-preserved Irish bog body of a male that was discovered in County Offaly, Republic of Ireland, while workmen were clearing a drainage ditch through a peat bog near the base of Croghan Hill in May 2003. The man is believed to have been murdered sometime between 362 and 175 BCE, which was at the height of the Celtic Iron Age. He was around twenty-years-old when he died, and the obvious signs of mutilation indicate that he had suffered a gruesome death. According to forensic analysis, the ill-fated nobleman had deep holes cut in both of his arms so that ropes could pass through them to restrain him. It appears he was then stabbed, cut in half, and had his nipples removed - prisoners and enemies defeated in battle would usually suck on the nipples of a king as a gesture of submission in pre-Christian Ireland, so the fact his nipples were cut off could mean that he was a disgraced ruler. The removal of nipples was usually done to signify that the person can never rule again - including in the afterlife. The plaited leather band around his left arm further indicates that he was a person of high importance. The man's body was naked except for the leather band, and investigators believe his final meal (analysed from the remaining contents found within his stomach) was a combination of wheat and buttermilk. He was also decapitated, but this was probably done after he had already been killed, and the most likely cause of death was a stab wound to the chest. One popular theory put forward is that the unfortunate man was sacrificed to the god of harvest to ensure the local population would have adequate amounts of food and avoid starvation. He was unearthed a little over two months after the discovery of another remarkably well-preserved male body known as the "Clonycavan Man" in County Meath in March 2003. The unique remains of both men are on display for the public to view at the National Museum of Ireland located in Dublin.

DID YOU KNOW?

"Cheddar Man" is the name given to Britain's oldest near-complete human skeleton. Discovered in 1903 by labourers digging a drainage ditch at Cheddar Gorge, Somerset, the skeletal remains belong to a young male who perished in his early 20s. It's estimated that he lived around the mid-to-late 9th millennium BCE, and was likely a Western European hunter-gatherer during the Mesolithic period. Fractures on the surface of his skull suggests he may have been murdered, although another hole in his skull could have been the result of a deadly infection. It's unclear how his remains came to be in the cave at Cheddar Gorge, but it's possible he was placed there by other members of his tribe after he had died. His remains are currently kept in the Human Evolution gallery inside London's Natural History Museum.

The Daily Mirror, 7th January 2006. "Murdered 2,500 Years Ago"

Timewatch: The Bog Bodies. **Series 25, Episode 7. TV Documentary (2006)**

Archeology Magazine, May-June 2010. "Clonycavan and Old Croghan Man"

The Irish Times, 4th June 2011. "Amulet, Old Croghan Man, 362-175 BC"

The Washington Post, 7th February 2018. "Meet Cheddar Man: First modern Britons had dark skin and blue eyes"

EARTH Magazine, 1st May 2018. "A new look at Cheddar Man"

WEDDING DAY DISASTER
ATTILA THE HUN
c. 406 - 453

Attila the Hun - also called the "scourge of God" - was ruler of the Hunnic Empire from 434 until his death in 453. He's considered to be one of the greatest barbarian rulers in history, having successfully expanded the empire of the Huns whilst achieving a high number of victories in key battles. Attila was thought to be unstoppable in combat, and he would've surely launched further campaigns against his enemies had he not died under mysterious circumstances on the night of his wedding. The conventional account provided by 5th century Greek historian and diplomat Priscus of Panium stated that Attila was attending a celebratory feast shortly after his wedding ceremony when he began to bleed heavily from his nose and mouth. Attila then apparently retreated to his private quarters, where he fell asleep under the influence of alcohol and started to choke on his own blood. He died in his sleep and was discovered the following morning by his servants. It's mostly assumed that he perished due to internal bleeding, which was probably caused by a rupture to the esophageal varices. The death of Attila led to the collapse of the Hun Empire. Those who had the misfortune of burying Attila's body were supposedly buried alive alongside him, so that the ruler's burial place would remain a secret. It's said that Attila's body was encased inside three separate coffins and buried in a tomb filled with the weapons and treasures of the rivals that he defeated in battle. No one knows the true location of where he is buried - several recent reports have claimed to have discovered his tomb, although these claims have all proven to be false.

"The Night Attila Died: Solving the Murder of Attila the Hun"
Michael A. Babcock (2005)
Rochas Revolution: Leadership by Example, **PP. 62-63. Nathaniel I. Ndiokwere (2012)**
Smithsonian Magazine, 3rd February 2012. "Nice Things to Say About Attila the Hun"
The Economic Times, 5th May 2016. "10 most ruthless leaders of all time"

A DEADLY TROPHY
SIGURD EYSTEINSSON
c. 832 - 892

The practice of warriors collecting human trophies has been evident during times of warfare throughout history, with the first documented instances dating back thousands of years. It involves the acquisition of human body parts - usually from the dead bodies of the enemy forces - that are used as decorative trophies. This is done for a variety of reasons, such as asserting dominance over the deceased or humiliating the opposition. Sigurd Eysteinsson (commonly referred to as Sigurd the Mighty) was the second Jarl of Orkney and a fierce combatant who typically collected the body parts of those that he vanquished in battle. The main sources for Sigurd's life are told in the old narrative Norse sagas *Heimskringla* and *Orkneyinga,* which depict him as a leading figure who played a crucial role during the Viking conquest of northern Scotland. The *Orkneyinga* saga claims that Sigurd challenged a well-known native ruler, Mael Brigte the Buck-Toothed, to a battle towards the end of his reign as Jarl of Orkney in 892. Brigte was swiftly defeated and beheaded by Sigurd, who then strapped the head of his foe to his horse's saddle as a trophy. Brigte's protruding back-tooth made contact with Sigurd's leg as he rode off however, causing a cut to open which became inflamed and infected. Sepsis quickly developed, and Sigurd would die from the affliction not long after sustaining the wound. It's said that his body was buried in a tumulus known as Sigurd's Howe. The exact location of his burial site is still currently unknown, although the most probable location is considered to be either modern-day Sidera or Cyderhall near Dornoch, which is located within the Scottish Highlands.

The Lore of Scotland: A Guide to Scottish Legends, **P 370. Jennifer Westwood & Sophia Kingshill (2009)**

Dreadful Fates, **P. 93. Tracey Turner (2010)**

Bitten to death by a dead man's head: The unfortunate, deserving & true tale of Sigurd Eysteinsson. **Stephen Liddell, 8th March 2004.**

The Orkney News, 19th March 2024. "Earl Sigurd I: The Mighty"

AN ILLICIT AFFAIR
POPE JOHN XII
c. 930/37 - MAY 14th 964

One can confidently assert that Pope John XII (originally known as Octavian) died doing what he loved - having sex. French historian and pamphleteer Louis Marie DeCormenin characterised the pope as "A robber, a murderer, and incestuous person, unworthy to represent Christ upon the pontifical throne… This abominable priest soiled the chair of St. Peter for nine entire years and deserved to be called the most wicked of popes." John was a slave to his passions and irresistible urges; he would often neglect his duties as bishop of Rome and ruler of the Papal States in favour of entertaining himself. The papal residence was said to have been a brothel during his reign, and legend has it that pagan rituals were regularly conducted in the Vatican. According to a written account by diplomat and bishop Liudprand of Cremona, John perished on 14 May 964 whilst indulging in an adulterous sexual encounter with a young married female somewhere outside of Rome. His cause of death was either the result of a fatal stroke as he engaged in sexual intercourse, or he was brutally murdered by the jealous husband of the woman - the outraged man supposedly strangled John and threw him out of a bedroom window. He went out with a bang whichever way he died, and his body was buried at the Basilica of San Giovanni in Laterano, Rome. Most modern scholars agree that he was an unfit pope whose papacy was notorious for its worldliness and depravity. Pope

Benedict V succeeded John, but his papacy lasted for only five weeks as he was successfully deposed by Leo VIII.

The Bad Popes, **PP. 955-963. Russell Chamberlin (2003)**

The deaths of the Popes: Comprehensive Accounts, Including Funerals, Burial Places and Epitaphs, **P. 72. Wendy J. Reardon (2015)**

The Independent, 24th September 2015. "7 wicked popes and the terrible, terrible things they did"

Time Magazine, 13th January 2017. "TV's Young Pope is scandalous, but the real youngest pope has the worst reputation"

A FALL FROM GRACE

CROWN PRINCE PHILIP OF FRANCE
AUGUST 29th 1116 - OCTOBER 13th 1131

Crown Prince Philip of France is not recognised by any ordinal or included in conventional lists of French monarchs, consequently because he predeceased his father, Louis VI of France, by six years and didn't reign as a sole king. Philip was the eldest son of King Louis VI (also called "Louis the Fat" for blatantly obvious reasons) and Adelaide of Maurienne. Born on 29 August 1116, he was named after his grandfather, Philip I, as was the traditional custom of naming the eldest son after their parental grandfathers. Philip was enthroned to rule alongside his father as co-king of France on 14 April 1129 at the age of twelve - a tradition that was implemented to reduce the likelihood of a younger sibling stepping forward upon their father's death to claim the crown and start a bitter civil war. Things would not go as intended for Philip, as he would perish in an unforeseen accident only two years after his coronation. The youngster had given his father a hard time since being elected as co-ruler, refusing to pay attention to his father's teachings and failing to implement the high standards that Louis VI had demonstrated throughout his life. Philip quickly became disobedient and did whatever he wanted; historic Welsh writer Walter Map stated that he "strayed from the paths of conduct travelled by his father and, by his overweening pride and tyrannical arrogance, made himself a burden to all." Perhaps Philip should've paid attention to his father's warnings instead of dismissing them. His brief reign as co-king came to an abrupt end on 13 October 1131, the day after he had suffered catastrophic injuries in Paris. The teenager had been riding horseback with a group of young companions near a section of the Seine River when a black pig suddenly darted out of a nearby dung heap and tripped his running horse. Philip was thrown off the horse so violently that he broke multiple bones when he landed on the ground, which likely included his neck or spinal cord. The impact knocked him out instantly, and his companions were quick to realise the severity of the situation for they rushed to get the paralysed Philip back to his home as soon as possible. He would die around twelve hours after the accident without ever regaining consciousness, and his body was buried at the Basilica of Saint-Denis in the northern suburbs of Paris. Philip had harboured a dream of visiting Jerusalem and the tomb of Jesus Christ whilst he was still alive; when he died - having never fulfilled this dream - his grieving brother, Louis VII of France, vowed to visit Jerusalem in his place. This promise gave Louis VII a reason to take part in the Second Crusade in 1147 as well as an excuse to disregard Antioch in favour of fully focusing on Jerusalem. The results of this decision were disastrous: The Second Crusade led to a huge loss of troops, and the abandonment of Antioch proved to be a partial cause for the failure of the king's marriage to his first wife Eleanor of Aquitaine. Philip's influence seemed to negatively affect the lives of all those around him, even in death.

DID YOU KNOW?

King William III of England (4 November 1650 - 8 March 1702) died in March 1702 as a result of the injuries he sustained when he fell from his horse after it had stumbled into a mole's burrow. William fractured his collarbone in the fall and contracted pneumonia not long afterwards, which claimed the king's life. Jacobites made an honorary toast for "the little gentleman in the black velvet waistcoat" to express their gratitude, as the animal had caused the demise of their arch-rival. Winston Churchill referred to the king's death in his volume of books *A History of the English-Speaking Peoples,* saying that William's fall had "opened the door to a troop of lurking foes". William was buried in Westminster Abbey alongside the body of his wife, Mary II of England, who had perished eight years previously in 1694. His sister-in-law and cousin Anne became Queen of England, Scotland and Ireland following his unexpected death.

The History of England from the Restoration to the Death of William III: 1660-1702, **P. 451. Sir Richard Lodge (1969)**

The Death of Kings: Royal Deaths in Medieval England, **PP. 49-50. Michael Evans (2003)**

Past Convictions: The Penance of Louis the Pious and the Decline of the Carolingians, **P. 79. Courtney M. Booker (2012)**

Blood Royal: Dynastic Politics in Medieval Europe, **P. 95. Robert Bartlett (2020)**

https://www.westminster-abbey.org/abbey-commemorations/royals/william-iii/

EXCESSIVE BRUTALITY
AL-MUSTA'SIM, THE LAST ABBASID CALIPH
1212/13 - FEBRUARY 20th 1258

Abu Ahmad Abdallah (better known as al-Musta'sim) was the 37th and last Abbasid caliph of Baghdad from 1242 until his brutal execution at the hands of Mongol invaders during the siege of Baghdad in February 1258. A large army under the command of Hulegu Khan, grandson of Genghis Khan and a prince of the Mongol Empire, attacked Baghdad and claimed the city within a few weeks. Al-Musta'sim had assembled a force of around 20,000 cavalry to defend the city from the Mongol army, but they were poorly equipped for the battle and were easily defeated. The Mongol forces then entered Baghdad on 13 February 1258, three days after the city had officially surrendered. Contemporary accounts state that the invading Mongol soldiers were exceptionally cruel and spared no one; citizens who attempted to flee the city were slaughtered, including countless women and children. Al-Musta'sim was captured by the invaders, who forced him to watch as his city burned and the people of Baghdad were viciously murdered. Hulegu thereafter declared that the caliph must be executed in a manner that would not offend the earth - the Mongols believed that spilling royal blood on the ground was a sin. There is wide disagreement among historians on the manner of his death, but the generally accepted account is that the Mongols decided to wrap the caliph up in a large rug and trample him with their horses until he died from multiple injuries (Marco Polo wrote that al-Musta'sim may have been starved to death after being locked away with his treasure, but this claim is considered to be historically inaccurate). The total death toll of the siege is estimated to have been around one million people, with Baghdad becoming a city of ruin. The stench of decaying bodies was so overwhelming that Hulegu was forced to relocate his troops upwind of the destroyed city.

Deadly Bloody Battles, **PP. 12-13. Madeline Donaldson (2013)**
The Guardian, 20th June 2014. "Baghdad: the psychological toll of being the world's most attacked city"
The Abbasid Caliphate, **P. 268. Tayeb El-Hibri (2021)**
The Horde: How the Mongols Changed the World, **PP. 142-143. Marie Favereau (2021)**

MYSTERIOUS ASSAILANTS
GIOVANNI BORGIA, 2ND DUKE OF GANDIA
c. 1476 - JUNE 14th 1497

The unsolved murder of Giovanni Borgia, 2nd Duke of Gandia, remains one of the most infamous scandals of the Borgia era in 15th Century Italy. The second child of Pope Alexander VI and Vannozza dei Cattanei, Giovanni was known to be the pope's preferred son, and he received favourable treatment as a result. No exact date of birth exists for him or his brother Cesare, and Giovanni was long thought to have been the couple's eldest son, but modern studies suggest that he must've been older than Cesare. Giovanni became the 2nd Duke of Gandia around the age of twelve in September 1488 following the death of his older half-brother Pier Luigi, and a marriage contract was hastily cobbled together for him to marry Maria Enriquez de Luna - the first cousin of King Ferdinand II of Aragon. The ceremony was ultimately postponed due to Giovanni's young age; however, the situation was eventually resolved four years later in 1492 when his father was elected pope and became known as Alexander VI. The long-awaited wedding took place after a political alliance was made between the papacy and the Crown of Aragon. Their marriage proved to be short-lived, as Giovanni was murdered by an unknown assailant on the night of 14 June 1497 in Rome. According to an account provided by the Alsatian-born chronicler Johann Burchard, Giovanni was last seen alive when he departed from his mother's house after having dinner with her. The duke informed his brother Cesare of his intentions to go and find entertainment somewhere in the company of his valet and unidentified masked man. The duke rode to the Square of the Jews in the Roman Ghetto, where he ordered his servant to wait for him. He told the servant he should return by 8 pm before he rode off with the masked man behind him on the back of his mule. When the duke failed to return to the Palace of Cardinal Ascanio Sforza (now known as the Palazzo Sforza Cesarini) the following morning on 15 June, his trusted servants became worried and went to the pope to inform him of Giovanni's failure to return home. The pope was deeply concerned by the news; although he convinced himself that his son was more than likely enjoying the company of a young female somewhere within the city. He desperately clung onto the hope that Giovanni would return by nightfall. The duke failed to show up throughout the entire day, and a search was initiated to locate him. The servant that Giovanni had instructed to wait for him at the Square of the Jews was found fatally injured and totally unresponsive; he soon died without giving any account of his master's fate, despite being taken into a house in the local area to receive care. Giovanni's mule returned to the palace - minus its owner - the very same day, with one of its stirrups cut. Alexander VI ordered that all houses on the banks of the Tiber River should be searched thoroughly, but the search failed to trace Giovanni's whereabouts. The duke would finally be located when a Slavonian timber dealer named Georgio came forward to make a statement. He claimed that he had been resting in his boat on the Tiber on the night of 14 June to protect his collection of wood when he witnessed five men throw a lifeless corpse into the river near The Hospital of Saint Jerome. Fishermen and boatmen were summoned to search the river, and Giovanni's body would be recovered shortly thereafter on 16 June. The duke had multiple wounds on his body, as his throat had been slit and eight other stab wounds were visible on his head, torso and legs. The pope locked himself away in his private chamber and wept for hours after the body was found. The identity of those that murdered Giovanni was never uncovered, and the case continues to pose unanswered questions centuries later.

Cesare Borgia: His Life and Times, **P. 17. Sarah Bradford (1976)**
Chronicle of the Popes, **PP. 158-159. P. G. Maxwell-Stuart (1997)**
The Borgias and Their Enemies, **P. 30. Christopher Hibbert (2008)**
Untimely Deaths by Assassination, **PP. 48-49. Walter J. Whittemore Jr (2012)**
Italy Magazine, 14th October 2013. "Italian Families: Borgia"
https://crimereads.com/cold-cases-of-history-the-murder-of-juan-borgia/

CUMNOR'S SECRET

AMY ROBSART

JUNE 7th 1532 - SEPTEMBER 8th 1560

Amy Robsart (later known as Lady Dudley) was the wife of Robert Dudley, a favorite of Queen Elizabeth I of England, who she married just prior to her eighteenth birthday in 1550. Their marriage began with promise, but as Robert rose in favor with Elizabeth, Amy's life took a turn toward isolation and obscurity. While Robert spent his days at court, Amy lived in the countryside, often separated from her husband for long periods of time. Her sudden death remains one of the most mysterious and debated events of the 16th century. She was found dead at the bottom of a staircase at Cumnor Place, her residence in Oxfordshire, on 8 September 1560. The circumstances surrounding her death were suspicious, and rumors quickly spread that she had been murdered, possibly to clear the way for Robert to marry Elizabeth (Dudley was widely believed to have ambitions to marry the queen, and killing his wife would have removed a significant obstacle). It was rumoured that the Queen had fallen in love with Dudley, and the speculation surrounding them only increased further when Elizabeth remained single. The official inquest into Amy's death ruled that it was an accident, suggesting she fell down the stairs. However, her neck was reportedly broken, and there were no visible injuries consistent with a fall, which fueled speculation that foul play had taken place - many contemporaries believed either Robert or Elizabeth was to blame. The staircase from which Robsart fell was relatively short, leading some to question whether it could have caused fatal injuries. The scandal ultimately damaged Robert Dudley's reputation and made it politically impossible for him to marry Queen Elizabeth, even though they had a close bond. Elizabeth would eventually distance herself from Dudley to protect her own image. Modern historians remain divided about that case; Some argue that Lady Dudley's death was indeed accidental, possibly due to illness (she was reported to have been suffering from a "malady in her breast," which some speculate could have been a form of cancer). Others suggest she may have taken her own life or been murdered by an unknown assailant - the lack of witnesses and the suspicious timing of her death lent credence to this theory. The suicide theory is not widely accepted though, as suicide was considered to be a grave sin at the time. Amy's body was buried at the University Church of St Mary the Virgin in Oxford on 22 September 1560, and it was said that her widower was in a state of deep mourning for six months after she died. Her perplexing death has inspired numerous literary works, including Sir Walter Scott's novel *Kenilworth* which immortalized her story and blended fact with fiction to create a romanticized version of her tragic end. The mysterious passing of lady Dudley endures as a fascinating chapter in Tudor history, and her unsolved death continues to captivate historians and the public alike.

Sweet Robin: A Biography of Robert Dudley Earl of Leicester 1533-1588, **PP. 118-120. Derek Wilson (1981)**

Amy Robsart: A life and its end, **PP. 7-9. Christine Hartweg (2017)**

English Heritage Magazine, 2nd February 2022. "Queen Elizabeth and Robert Dudley: The Real Story"

Retrospect Journal, 23rd October 2022. "Tudor True Crime: The Bizarre Death of Amy Dudley"

Not Just The Tudors: The Death of Amy Dudley. **Apple Podcast (2023)**

TREAD CAREFULLY
HANS STEININGER
1508 - SEPTEMBER 28th 1567

There is a large stone relief of a gentleman with an unusually long beard that stretches down past his feet displayed on the side of St. Stephen's Church in the small town of Braunau am Inn on the Austrian-German border. The epitaph is dedicated to Hans Steininger, the "man with the very long beard" who served as burgomaster (town mayor) of Braunau am Inn during the mid-16th century. His extraordinarily long beard, measuring approximately 1.4 meters in length (around 4.5 feet) was a symbol of pride to Steininger, and it became a standout feature of his appearance. He usually kept it rolled up and tucked inside a pouch to avoid it interfering with his day-to-day life, but he seemingly forgot to conceal his beard on 28 September 1567, and it had disastrous consequences for the mayor. A large fire broke out in the town hall that caused a general panic as people hurried towards the exits. Steininger helped to organise rescue efforts before he attempted to escape from the burning structure. His beard was hanging free as he ran through the flames, and he managed to step on it in the midst of the chaos, sending him plummeting down a flight of stairs. The fall was so severe that Steininger broke his neck, killing him instantly. News of his bizarre death spread all across Europe, with the story being recounted for its strange circumstances. Steininger's beard was cut off after he died and given to his close relatives, who passed it down from generation to generation as a family heirloom until they donated it to the local museum in 1919. The beard still remains on display behind a glass cabinet at the Bezirksmuseum Herzogsburg museum located in Braunau am Inn.

The Art of Growing a Beard, **P. 47. Marvin Grosswirth (2014)**
What the Fact?!, **P. 222. Gabe Henry (2018)**
Ammon News, 4th November 2021. "Humanity's unluckiest ever deaths - from severed cobra heads to laughing fits"
"The man who was killed by his own beard" **29th March 2023.**
Mike Rampton.
https://allthatsinteresting.com/hans-steininger

STAYING IN CHARACTER
MOLIERE (BORN JEAN-BAPTISTE POQUELIN)
JANUARY 16th 1622 (BAPTISED) - FEBRUARY 17th 1673

Moliere is considered to be one of the greatest comic geniuses that the world has ever seen, and he is certainly a master of social comedy. The French playwright, actor, and poet had a long volume of work that ranged from straightforward farces to sophisticated satires, including his most enduring plays *Tartuffe* and *Le Misanthrope*. He is held in such high regard that the French language is often referred to as the "language of Moliere". Moliere took the starring role in all of the plays he wrote; his favourite characters to portray were usually jealous lovers or bitter husbands to create comedic storylines that would provoke a satisfactory reaction from the crowd. It is often said that he passed away while performing in the title-role of his play *The Hypochondriac* (also known as *The Imaginary Invalid*) on 17 February 1673. Moliere was known to suffer from pulmonary tuberculosis, something which he likely contracted during the time he spent in prison as a young man. The more widely accepted account is that Moliere was seized by a coughing fit and collapsed on-stage; he quickly improvised and managed to finish his performance, but he then experienced a large hemorrhage and collapsed again once he left the stage. He was quickly carried to his home in the Rue de Richelieu section of Paris, where he died within the hour without receiving the last rites. Two priests refused to perform the last rites because Moliere was an actor (they were perceived badly by the Catholic Church during that time period), while a third priest arrived too late. King Louis XIV allowed for the playwright's body to be buried on the sacred ground of a cemetery - something that wasn't permitted under 17th Century law. His remains were relocated to Pere Lachaise Cemetery in Paris in 1817.

The White Death: A History of Tuberculosis, **P. 10. Thomas Dormandy (2000)**

Moliere: A Theatrical Life, **P. 256. Virginia Scott (2002)**

Moliere, the French Revolution, and the Theatrical Afterlife, **PP. 110-111. Mechele Leon (2009)**

America Magazine, 6th January 2023. "French playwright Moliere's fraught relationship with the Catholic Church: A fresh look on his 400th birthday"

DON'T PROVOKE THE BEAST
HANNAH TWYNNOY
c. 1670 - OCTOBER 23rd 1703

There is a centuries-old headstone on the grounds of Malmesbury Abbey Cemetery in Wiltshire that commemorates an early 18th century British bar worker named Hannah Twynnoy, who is allegedly the first person to be mauled to death by a tiger in the United Kingdom. Her epitaph reads: "In bloom of life she's snatch'd from hence, she had not room to make her defence; for tyger fierce took life away. And here she lies in a bed of clay, until the resurrection day". Twynnoy worked at The White Lion public house in the market district of Malmesbury, and it's said that she was slain by a tiger that was housed at the pub alongside other wild animals for the purpose of public exhibitions. She apparently teased the tiger while it was loosely connected to a wall in the pub garden, causing it to become increasingly agitated. It managed to break free from its flimsy shackles and lunged at Twynnoy. She was quickly torn apart by the large animal - the tiger's keeper was seemingly nowhere in sight. Very little is known about Twynnoy, other than her role of employment and that she was aged thirty-three at the time of her death. Author John Marks Moffat provided a detailed account of her death in his book *History of Malmesbury* (1805), whilst the Athelstan Museum contains an undated letter from an unknown person that describes Twynnoy's story and quotes the epitaph that is written on her headstone. The inscription on her headstone became almost impossible to read after many years of neglect, which prompted the locals of Malmesbury to launch a fundraising campaign that successfully generated enough money to hire masonry restorers who were able to clean up the gravesite in late 2024. The site where The White Lion pub was located at 8 Gloucester Street is now a private household.

The Wiltshire Gazette and Herald, 23rd October 2003. "Riddle of the savaged serving maid lives on"

The Daily Telegraph, 24th September 2007. "BBC reveals Britain's most unusual epitaphs"

Wiltshire and Gloucestershire Standard, 28th September 2007. "Is this Britain's strangest gravestone?"

Dreadful Fates, **P. 47. Tracey Turner (2010)**

The Times, 7th June 2016. "Wanted: Historians to fill in national knowledge gaps"

Nature is the Worst: 500 Reasons You'll Never Want To Go Outside Again, **P. 176. E. Reid Ross (2017)**

BBC News, 11th October 2024. "Tiger victim's 18th Century headstone restored in Malmesbury"

RIDE THE LIGHTNING
GEORG WILHELM RICHMANN
JULY 22nd 1711 - AUGUST 6th 1753

Russian physicist Georg Wilhelm Richmann (of Baltic German origin) became famous for establishing the first general equation for calorimetric calculations. The brilliant scientist did vast amounts of pioneering scientific work on electricity, atmospheric forms of electricity, and calorimetry throughout the duration of his career. He was also well-known for the investigations he conducted on thunderstorm electricity - one of these risky experiments would cost Richmann his life and almost kill his assistant. He was fatally electrocuted in Saint Petersburg on 6 August 1753 while conducting an electrical investigation during a humid thunderstorm, which involved "trying to quantify the response of an insulated rod to a nearby storm" at Richmann's household. It's widely reported that the scientist had been attending an important meeting with members of the Academy of Sciences when he heard the sound of approaching thunder, at which point he sensed an opportunity to obtain noteworthy scientific data and he abruptly left the meeting to return home with his personal engraver to prepare for the experiment. As the proceedings got underway, an electrical discharge - said to have been ball lightning - suddenly materialized inside the room and struck Richmann directly in the centre of his forehead. The impact left a large red dot on his face, blew his left shoe wide open, and singed parts of his clothing; he died almost instantly after being hit by the electrical current. A subsequent explosion tore the room's door off its hinges and rendered the unnamed assistant unconscious. Richmann is speculated to be the first person in history to have perished while conducting electrical experiments.

The Pennsylvania Gazette, 5th March 1754.
Ball Lightning: An Unsolved Problem in Atmospheric Physics, **P. 75. Mark Stenhoff (1999)**
From Clouds to the Brain: The Movement of Electricity in Medical Science, **P. 91. Celine Cherici (2020)**
Spark: The Life of Electricity and the Electricity of Life, **P. 19. Timothy J. Jorgensen (2023)**

BENDING THE RULES
CROWN PRINCE SADO
FEBRUARY 13th 1735 - JULY 12th 1762

Unloved by his father since the day he was born, Crown Prince Sado (personal name Yi Seon) grew up to be a very disturbed man. He was the second son of King Yeongjo of Joseon, and the young price would've become the future monarch - due to the premature death of his older half-brother, Crown Prince Hyojanghad, in 1728 - had his tyrannical behaviour not led to his downfall at the age of twenty-seven. Sado was very superstitious and exceptionally brutal, for he took pleasure in murdering his servants whenever he felt agitated or depressed. He killed people with such regularity that several dead bodies had to be removed from the Changgyeong Palace on a daily basis. On one occasion he walked into his private chambers holding the severed head of a eunuch and demanded the ladies-in-waiting and his wife, Lady Hyegyong, look at it (this incident is recounted by Hyegyong in her memoir entitled *Memories of Lady Hyegyong*, which provides in-sight details into Sado's chaotic life). Sado even killed one of his favourite concubines named Bing-ae - who had birthed several of his children - in 1761 after he flew into a fit of rage while getting dressed. Various reports claim he also tried to seduce his younger sister, Princess Hwawan, and threatened to slash her with his sword when she resisted his advances. The entire royal family was afraid that the depraved prince was going to end up killing one if not all of them, so Yeongjo was forced to take drastic action. The king had to find a suitable solution; a royal body couldn't be defiled (executed) under court law, and the then-common practice of communal punishment meant that any punishment handed down to Sado would also have to be carried out on his innocent wife and son - the family's only direct male heir. Yeongjo had no desire to execute or banish his grandson, nor did he wish to tarnish his own reputation. To resolve this issue, he summoned Sado to the royal palace on 5 July 1762 and stripped him of all his titles. Yeongjo then ordered him to climb into a small wooden rice chest. Sado's pleas for mercy fell on deaf ears, and he was forcibly placed into the chest in front of his wife. Several of his eunuchs and workmen were put to death in the palace on that day as well. Sado's narrow prison had to be tightly sealed with rope after he attempted to climb back out, and he was left to starve to death. He continued to respond from inside the chest until the night of 11 July; he was pronounced dead after the chest was opened the following day, probably due to a lack of water. Yeongjo decided to restore his son to the position of crown prince after he passed away, and also gave him the title Sado - which means "thinking of with great sorrow". Sado's son, Chong-Jo, acceded the Korean throne in 1776, and he would go on to become known as one of Korea's greatest-ever king's. Modern historians tend to have a more sympathetic view towards Sado, as the constant abuse he received as a child undoubtedly played a major role in the deterioration of his mental health.

Brief History: Brief History of Korea, **P. 114. Mark Peterson (2009)**

The Korea Times, 27th November 2009. "Book reconstitutes secret of Prince Sado's death"

The Memoirs of Lady Hyegyong: The Autobiographical Writings of a Crown Princess of Eighteenth-Century Korea, **PP. 324-325. JaHyun Kim Kim Haboush & Dorothy Ko (2013)**

Korea JoongAng Daily, 14th October 2015. "The ever-changing history of Prince Sado"

The Analects of Dasan: A Korean Syncretic Reading Volume II, **P. 219. Yag-yong Chong (2016)**

Past Forward: Essays in Korean History, **PP. 65-67. Kyung Moon Hwang (2019)**

HUNTING FOR A GHOST
THOMAS MILLWOOD
1781 - JANUARY 3rd 1804

The Hammersmith Ghost murder case is a classic tale of hoaxes and mass hysteria that plagued the residents of Hammersmith, West London, during the final months of 1803. A ghostly apparition was reportedly sighted by multiple men and women as they made their way through the district at night. Some witnesses said the ghost was attired in a white sheet, whilst others said that it wore some kind of animal skin. When the story was reported in the local newspapers - similar to how the Plaistow Ghost incident would unfold years later in 1889 - it caused a sensation, and rumours that the ghost in question was the spirit of a man who had killed himself the year before began circulating amongst the population of Hammersmith. The man had apparently been buried in the local churchyard, which was forbidden by church law at the time (as suicide was considered to be a sin against God) and therefore made him a likely suspect in the eyes of the hysterical residents. It wasn't long before night patrols were set up around the borough to keep watch, as groups of young men armed themselves with pistols and rifles for protection while they wandered the dark lanes of Hammersmith at night to locate the menacing spectre. One of the patrolmen would eventually stumble upon the very thing that he was hunting, or so he thought. Twenty-nine-year-old excise officer Francis Smith encountered a figure dressed in white clothing at the corner of Beavor Lane during a routine patrol on 3 January 1804, and he immediately suspected that it was the ghost. The figure was actually a bricklayer named Thomas Millwood who was dressed in the normal white clothing of his trade. Millwood was on his way home after visiting family members at their house in Black Lion Lane, and his sister, Anne Millwood, would hear Smith confront her brother shortly after he departed. She claimed that Smith said: "Damn you; who are you and what are you? Damn you, I'll shoot you." Smith then aimed his shotgun at Millwood and fired. The bricklayer was killed almost instantly when the bullet struck him in his lower left jaw. A constable would arrive on the scene after hearing the gunshot and promptly took Smith into custody. He was charged with wilful murder as he had killed an unarmed man. Smith refuted the charge nonetheless; he claimed that he had acted in self-defence, and the ghost proved he was an apparition by not stopping when ordered to - why Smith thought that bullets would halt the ghost in its tracks was not addressed. Smith was sentenced to death by hanging for the crime, with his body to be dissected at a later date (a common practice on executed criminals during the early 19th century). However, the judge presiding over the case reported it to King George III, who had the power to commute the sentence if he wished to do so. Smith got lucky as the original punishment was overruled, and he served one year's hard labour instead. An elderly shoemaker named John Graham came forward to confess that he was the person who had been dressing up as a ghost and scaring the locals after the court case had reached its conclusion. He felt partly responsible for

Millwood's death, so he chose to tell the police about his disruptive shenanigans. There is no official record of Graham ever being punished.

The Proceedings of the Old Bailey, 11th January 1804. "Francis Smith, Killing"

Kirby's Wonderful and Scientific Museum, **PP. 65-79. R.S. Kirby (1804)**

Crime Magazine, 9th April 2015. "The Hammersmith Ghost and the Strange Death of Thomas Millwood"

Apparitions Or The Mystery of Ghosts, **PP. 89-90. Joseph Taylor (2018)**

Londonist Magazine, 25th October 2019. "The time someone shot a ghost dead in Hammersmith"

After Dark: Myths, Misdeeds & the Paranormal. Hammersmith Ghost: How to Murder a Poltergeist. **Ep. 10. Podcast (2023)**

A GROTESQUE PROCEDURE
GOUVERNEUR MORRIS
JANUARY 31st 1752 - NOVEMBER 6th 1816

Gouverneur Morris, author of the *Preamble to the United States Constitution* and widely referred to as the "Penman of the Constitution", was one of the lesser-known founding fathers of the United States. Morris famously advanced the idea of Americans becoming a citizen of a single union of states at a time when most of the population still regarded themselves to be citizens of their own respective states. It's a mighty shame that Morris is more commonly remembered for the way he died instead of the vital contributions he made in helping to establish the United States. The outspoken slavery opponent and former New York senator met a strange end after he critically injured himself, as Morris naively tried to solve his own health problem instead of consulting a physician. His health had begun to drastically decline by 1816, so he started to experiment with various remedies in a last-ditch bid to improve his own wellbeing. He developed a painful blockage in his urinary tract that same year, and it gradually became worse when he refused to seek medical treatment. Morris eventually opted to try and clear the blockage himself by using a piece of whale baleen from his wife's corset as a makeshift catheter - some reports claim that this gruesome procedure was successful in removing the blockage. In any case, the self-surgery caused substantial internal injuries and led to further complications. Morris's inner tissue had been torn and quickly became inflamed, from which he developed a serious penile infection. The infection would claim his life - ironically in the exact same room that his mother had given birth to him in - on 6 November 1816 at the age of sixty-four. He died in the company of his relatives at the family estate in Morrisania, and his body was later transferred to New York City to be buried at St. Ann's Episcopal Church located in The Bronx. The American liberty ship *SS Gouverneur Morris* was built in 1943 to serve in World War II and is named in his honour.

DID YOU KNOW?

19th century British surgeon Robert Liston had a (befitting) reputation of being the fastest surgeon in the world during his era - it's said that he could amputate a limb in under a minute. He was considered to be a skilled surgeon with a somewhat argumentative personality. Despite his many achievements, Liston is often remembered in the modern age due to a couple of horrendous blunders he made during surgical procedures. He holds the distinction of being the only surgeon in known history to have a 300% mortality rate for a single operation. The patient that Liston was operating on later died of an infection, as did his young assistant whose fingers were accidentally amputated by the surgeon, and a spectator died of shock when Liston's knife slashed his clothing. Another mishap occurred on a separate occasion when Liston unintentionally castrated a patient who was there to have a leg amputated.

The National Intelligencer, 12th November 1816. "Gouverneur Morris Death"

The City Journal, 1st April 2002. "The Forgotten Founding Father" Scandal At Bizarre: Rumor and Reputation in Jefferson's America,

P. 145. Cynthia A. Kierner (2006)

The Boston Globe, 12th May 2012. "The surgery with a 300% mortality rate"

The Washington Post, 31st October 2017. "Screams, torture and so much blood: The gruesome world of 19th-Century surgery"

Time Magazine, 1st July 2022. "Beyond the Founding Fathers: 12 Unsung Figures Who Helped Build America"

Amplitude Magazine, 5th July 2023. "The Down-Low on America's Amputee Founding Father"

A WAYWARD SHOT
MELVINA ELLEN NASON BUTLER
AUGUST 13th 1861 - SEPTEMBER 2nd 1884

American housewife Melvina Butler was busy making pies at her home in East Boston on 2 September 1884 when a stray bullet entered through the kitchen window and fatally struck her. The shot came from Navy Private John C. Murrey, who was stationed at Charleston Navy Yard which was approximately one mile away from Butler's home. Murrey had fired his weapon in the direction of approaching pirates - who were looking to steal materials - to warn them off, but the shot was horribly wayward and the bullet flew in the direction of Butler's house instead. She was bending over to lift her pies out of the oven as the bullet hit her directly in her left breast. The impact of the .50 calibre round caused her body to rise several feet into the air before she slammed against the kitchen floor. Butler, aged twenty-three, died within minutes, even though her husband valiantly attempted to preserve her life. The local police department launched an investigation and managed to trace the origin of the bullet back to Private Murrey. He was swiftly arrested and charged with murder, despite his insistence that Butler's death was a terrible accident. It also appears that he was simply obeying orders when he discharged his firearm at the navy yard, as his superiors ordered him to shoot close to where the pirates were positioned in the river should they choose to ignore the navy's verbal warnings. Murrey was also apparently given permission to fire directly at the pirates if all other measures failed to deter them. Information is almost non-existent regarding whether Private Murrey was actually sentenced or not in relation to the death of Melvina Butler, so his fate remains unknown.

The New York Times, 3rd September 1884. "A Rifle's Long Shot. A sentry's bullet kills a woman a mile away"

The Lancaster Examiner, 10th September 1884. "Shot by a sentry"

The Shepherdstown Register, 12th September 1884. "Shot dead in her kitchen"

Oneida Free Press, 16th September 1884. "Shot by a marine"

A RUDE AWAKENING
SAMUEL WARDELL
c. 1841 - DECEMBER 31st 1885

Samuel Wardell was a humble 19th century lamplighter from New York City who, like so many other inventors, was killed by his own creation. Wardell wasn't a genius by any means, although he was able to devise a unique wake-up system that would ensure he was never late for work. Lamplighters had a tight schedule that they had to adhere to; their job required them to light a city's gaslights at dusk and extinguish them at the break of dawn. An article in the *Democrat and Chronicle* published on 2 January 1886 stated that "On the top of his clock he (Wardell) adjusted a heavy stone, so nearly evenly balanced that the natural shaking of the bell would cause it to roll off to the floor and thus awaken the sleeper by its crash." It was a primitive device, but it did the job it was intended to do nonetheless - until it killed him during the festive season in 1885. A christmas party was thrown at Wardell's residence in Flatbush while he was absent, and his housemates relocated his bed from its usual spot to make suitable space for the attending guests. They just so happened to place the bed beneath the clock that held the heavy stone in place - something Wardell failed to notice when he returned home to sleep after the party had ended. The alarm clock went off as it was supposed to a few hours later, and the unlucky lamplighter was struck directly on the skull by the heavy stone while he was still sleeping. Wardell was taken to Kings County Hospital in Brooklyn to receive emergency medical treatment for his serious head injuries. There was little that could be done to save him however, and he would die on 31 January 1885 after spending three days in the hospital.

The New York Sun, 1st January 1886. "Mr. Wardell's Fatal Alarm Clock"

Democrat and Chronicle, 2nd January 1886. "Killed By His Own Invention"

The Representative (Fox Lake, Wisconsin), 13th January 1886. "A Singular Death"

Wordpress: "Inventive Deaths - How to Die in a Better Mousetrap", **2nd August 2018.**

CASTING OUT DEMONS
MOSES HOAKIMOA
c. 1840 – APRIL 1903

Having a bible repeatedly whacked on the top of your head doesn't exactly sound like the typical treatment you'd expect to receive for having a high fever, but that's exactly what a kahuna (shaman) named Kahuna Makaio did to the elderly and frail Hawaiian native Moses Hoakimoa in the Puna district of Hawaii in April 1903. His unorthodox method of violently assaulting Hoakimoa with the holy book would inadvertently end up killing the bedridden man. Makaio was called upon by Hoakimoa after the sick old man grew dissatisfied with the medical treatment he was receiving from government physician Dr. J. Holland, as he didn't think that Holland's remedies were curing his illness fast enough. Makaio discarded the medicines and came to the conclusion that Hoakimoa was possessed by multiple demons, with prayer being prescribed as a potential cure. Hoakimoa was far too weak to stand on his feet, so the kahuna ordered him to sit up in bed instead. Makaio then struck the sick man over and over again on the head with a bible for a few minutes until his arm grew tired, at which point he asked Hoakimoa's wife to carry on striking her husband's head with the bible while he regained his energy. She gladly accepted the task, and her husband fell unconscious in his bed after she dealt multiple blows. The procedure was repeated a few days later; this time Hoakimoa didn't survive the further blows he took to his head.

Makaio was initially arrested on the charge of witchcraft, and he was sentenced to two years of hard labour at Oahu Prison after being found guilty of manslaughter by a grand jury. Dr. Holland testified in court that the excessive blows inflicted upon Hoakimoa caused his heart to fail due to shock.

The Hawaiian Star, 2nd May 1903. "Beaten to death with a bible: A Kahuna in Puna tries to cast out devils with a fatal result"
The Minneapolis Journal, 10th July 1903. "Kahuna in Hawaii"
The Hawaiian Gazette, 21st July 1903. "Kahuna talks of his trade"
Wordpress: "Violent Kahuna Therapy?" **5th September 2015.**

THE PUPPET KING
ALEXANDER OF GREECE
AUGUST 1st 1893 - OCTOBER 25th 1920

The second son of King Constantine I, Alexander became king of Greece on 11 June 1917 after his father had been pushed to abdicate. He was effectively imprisoned within his own palace by the Venizelists when he ascended to the throne however, as the new king was young and had no prior political experience - thus he was reduced to the status of a puppet king. Alexander's reign only lasted for a little over three years before he died on 25 October 1920 at the age of twenty-seven from sepsis, as the wounds he suffered in a sustained attack by a Barbary macaque became infected. Alexander had been injured by the monkey three weeks earlier as he was taking a stroll through the grounds of the Taroi estate. The king's German Shepherd dog (named Fritz) either attacked or was attacked by a domesticated monkey - who belonged to a steward of the palace - and Alexander desperately tried to separate the animals as they fought. As he was preoccupied with breaking up the animals, another monkey attacked Alexander and bit him several times on his leg and torso. Servants at the palace heard the commotion and quickly rushed to chase away the monkeys. The king asked those who came to his aid to not publicise the incident as he didn't deem the incident to be serious enough to warrant unnecessary attention. Alexander's wounds were appropriately cleaned at the palace, although he refused to have them cauterised - a measure that might have saved his life. His wounds got infected later that evening; a strong fever overcame him and sepsis set in. His personal physicians briefly considered amputating his leg, yet none of them wanted to take responsibility and carry out the daunting task. This lack of decisive action by his doctors led to Alexander passing away twenty-three days after he sustained the monkey bites. His body was interred on the grounds of the royal palace at Tatoi. The Greek royal family never regarded Alexander's reign to be fully legitimate because he was mostly controlled by the Greek government during World War I. Constantine I would eventually be restored to the throne for his second term on 19 December 1920 following a referendum.

DID YOU KNOW?

An elderly pensioner from India was stoned to death by a hostile group of monkeys as he was collecting drywood in October 2018. Dharampal Singh, aged seventy-two, was going about his business in Tikri, Uttar Pradesh, when the monkeys started throwing bricks at him from a nearby tree. The volatile animals had reportedly collected the bricks from a dilapidated building nearby, and Singh was struck on the head and chest as the concrete blocks rained down on him from above. Singh was rushed to a local hospital where he died a short time later. The local police department declared that the elderly man's death was an accident, and they refused to take legal action against the monkeys. "How can we register the case against monkeys?" said police officer Chitwan Singh.

The Portsmouth Herald, 14th October 1920. "Monkey Bites King of Greece"

The Leeds Mercury, 26th October 1920. "Greek King Dies"

The Times, 2nd November 1920. "Royal Funeral in Athens"

The First World War Peace Settlements, 1919-1925, **P. 61. Erik Goldstein (2013)**

The Independent, 29th October 2018. "Man 'stoned to death by monkeys' in India"

Historical Dictionary of Modern Greece, **P. 26. Dimitris Keridis (2022)**

A SHROUDED END
OTTAVIO BOTTECCHIA
AUGUST 1st 1894 - JUNE 14th 1927

The death of Ottavio Bottecchia - the first Italian cyclist to wear the coveted yellow jersey in the Tour de France - remains one of the most enigmatic episodes in the long history of cycling, shrouded in speculation and multiple conspiracy theories. Bottecchia was a humble bricklayer turned cycling champion who rose to fame in the early 1920s, winning stages at the Tour de France and finishing second overall in 1923 before he claimed the title in 1924 and 1925. He quickly became a national hero, although his outspoken anti-fascist views and modest working-class roots also made him an enemy of the powerful and growing National Fascist Party led by Benito Mussolini. Bottecchia was found unconscious by a farmer near a field close to Peonis, a small village in northeastern Italy, on 3 June 1927 - the cyclist had gone out alone earlier that day to train in preparation for the 1927 edition of the Tour de France. He had severe head injuries and a fractured collarbone, and his bicycle was located some distance away, undamaged. Locals carried the stricken Bottecchia to an inn, and a priest arrived shortly thereafter to give him the last rites. He was then taken to Gemona Hospital where he died on 14 June 1927 without ever regaining consciousness. Some theorised that the farmer who had discovered Bottecchia had actually murdered the cyclist with a rock after he had caught him stealing some of his grapes, but grapes are usually too sour to eat at that time of year. Others said that he was killed by members of the powerful fascist party due to his critical assessment of the regime. The police later returned a verdict of accidental death, presumably caused by a freak accident of some kind - the suspicious police report was never fully verified, and the truth behind his death remains a mystery. A monument was erected near the location where he was discovered in 2000, commemorating his contributions to cycling.

Tour de France/Tour de Force: A Visual History of the World's Greatest Bicycle Race, **P. 41. James Startt (2000)**
Outside Magazine, 1st November 2006. "What really killed this Tour de France champion?"
Cycling News, 9th March 2007. "Cycling's Murder Mysteries"
Smithsonian Magazine, 19th November 2012. "Tycho Brahe probably wasn't murdered, but these people were"
The Times, 21st June 2024. "Remarkable life and mysterious death of Italy's first Tour de France winner"
Outside Magazine, 28th June 2024. "Tales of the Unexpected: Italy's First Tour de France start is the 100th anniversary of it's first tour champion"

CHEAT THE HANGMAN
WILLIAM KOGUT
c. 1904 – OCTOBER 20th 1930

Convicted killer William Kogut avoided execution by taking matters into his own hands on 17 October 1930 while he was incarcerated at Folsom State Prison in California. Kogut, a logger by trade, was a twenty-six-year-old Polish immigrant who had been found guilty of murdering a middle-aged landlady named Mayme Guthrie - it's rumoured that her boarding house doubled as a seedy brothel and gaming room - in Oroville, California, on 29 May 1930. Kogut claimed he had been drinking at the time and had no recollection of killing Guthrie, which he did by cutting her throat with a small pocket knife. He was sentenced to death for the shocking crime; however, he would die before he could reach the gallows. The death row inmate constructed a makeshift explosive device using a deck of playing cards and matches as he sat in his cell. He inserted match heads into the cards, rolled them tightly, and placed them inside of a hollowed-out piece of his bunk bed. Kogut then filled the space with water, creating pressure that caused the device to explode. Fragments of the pipe bomb got stuck in his face, and a portion of his skull was blown off in the blast. A suicide note written by Kogut and addressed to the prison warden was found in his cell which read: "Don not blame my death on anyone, because I fixed everything myself. I never give up as long as I am living, but this is the end." He died in the prison's hospital wing three days later, and his death is an example of the desperation that can arise in ruthless prison environments.

Healdsburg Tribune, 20th October 1930. "Death felon cheats rope with suicide"

Oroville Mercury Register, 20th October 1930. "Local man's suicide try successful"

The Baraboo News (Wisconsin), 20th October 1930. Prisoner victim of home made bomb"

The 1930s death row inmate who killed himself with a bomb made from a pack of playing cards. **Andrew Martin, 23rd November 2022.**

EXTREME AIR RAGE
LEONARD GEORGE KOENECKE
JANUARY 18th 1904 – SEPTEMBER 17th 1935

American baseball player Len Koenecke went into a complete meltdown in the wake of being cut from the Brooklyn Dodgers squad roster on 16 September 1935. Koenecke's recent on-field performances had been poor, and he was informed of his exclusion from the team after they had just arrived in St. Louis to participate in a National League game against the St. Louis Cardinals. Koenecke quickly departed to catch a flight back to New York City - it was the last time his teammates would see him alive. The outfielder boarded an American Airlines flight bound for New York City via Chicago and Detroit, with Koenecke contacting his wife at their in-season Brooklyn apartment by telephone before he boarded the flight to inform her that he would be home shortly. He had appeared to have taken the news that his season was over philosophically at first; however, he soon began to spiral out of control. Although not previously known to have been a drinker, Koenecke appeared to be visibly drunk at the airport in St. Louis, and he had a bottle of whisky in his possession when he entered the aircraft. The flight to Chicago was uneventful; nonetheless problems arose during the trip to Detroit. Koenecke started to argue with fellow passengers before he struck a female stewardess named Eleanor Woodard when she tried to de-escalate the situation. He then challenged another passenger to a fist fight, which forced the aircraft's co-pilot, R.C.

Pickering, to detain and guard over Koenecke for the remainder of the flight. He was taken off the plane by airline officials upon landing in Detroit, with his fare to New York refunded. Still resoundingly drunk, the baseball player fell asleep across a row of chairs after he staggered into the airport lounge. Koenecke woke up just after midnight and came across charter flight pilot William Mulqueeney in the terminal, who agreed to fly Koenecke back to Buffalo in the company of his friend Irwin Davis. The flight initially proceeded without issue, until Koenecke started to nudge Mulqueeney on the shoulder as he piloted the plane. Mulqueeney ordered him to knock it off (Koenecke refused to do so) and to sit at the back of the fuselage. Koenecke then became aggressive and started to physically attack the much smaller Davis, who was quickly overpowered by the stronger baseballer. Now completely unhinged, Koenecke attempted to seize control of the plane from Mulqueeney. The two men fought as the aircraft lurched through the sky. In an act of sheer desperation, Mulqueeney bashed Koenecke over the head several times with the on-board fire extinguisher - leaving him bleeding and unresponsive on the cabin floor. Mulqueeney subsequently made an emergency landing in the Toronto suburb of Etobicoke, with Koenecke's lifeless body located in the rear of the passenger compartment. An autopsy of his body revealed that the cause of death was a cerebral haemorrhage caused by the hard blows he received. An inquest laid the blame solely on Koenecke; the jury was satisfied that both Mulqueeney and Davis had acted justifiably in self-defence as Koenecke had been intoxicated, and no criminal charges were brought against either man.

DID YOU KNOW?

Nineteen-year-old Las Vegas resident Jonathan Burton was killed by fellow passengers aboard Southwest Airlines Flight 1763 on route to Salt Lake City International Airport from McCarran International Airport in Paradise, Nevada, on 11 August 2000 after he stormed the cockpit of the aircraft while in-flight. The disgruntled teenager was subdued by around six to eight other passengers, but they applied such a tremendous amount of force onto Burton's neck that he died from suffocation. No one was charged in relation to his death, and there was no obvious reason as to why Burton had the sudden outburst. He had no prior history of mental health issues, nor had he ever exhibited violent tendencies before. Investigators also determined that the levels of cocaine and marijuana present in his body at the time of his death were too low to be considered a contributing factor towards his unusual behaviour.

The New York Times, 18th September 1935. "Len Koenecke killed on airplane"

The Guardian, 23rd September 2000. "Passenger 'mob' killed air rage man"

The Globe and Mail, 17th September 2005. "The strange, sordid death of a ballplayer"

Shortened Seasons: The untimely deaths of Major League baseball stars and journeymen, **PP. 26-28. Fran Zimniuch (2007)** Baseball's Most Notorious Personalities, **PP. 16-18. Jonathan Weeks (2013)**

LIVED ONCE, DIED TWICE
MARCUS MOSIAH GARVEY
AUGUST 18th 1887 - JUNE 10th 1940

A death hoax is a deliberate report of someone's death - usually a celebrity or a public figure of high importance - that is later revealed to be factually incorrect, and there are many instances of people who have mistakenly been reported to be dead in recent history. Take the case of Marcus Garvey for example, whose death was splashed across the pages of various British newspapers when he was in fact still alive - although not for much longer. The Jamaican-born social activist was a controversial figure during his lifetime; he identified himself as a Black nationalist and Pan-Africanist who held a strong belief that Black members of society needed to become financially independent from largely White-dominated societies. He founded the Universal Negro Improvement Association and African Communities League (commonly known as UNIA) in July 1914 after arriving back in Jamaica from the United Kingdom, and his political ideas came to be known as Garveyism. For all his brilliance as an activist, Garvey struggled with multiple ailments throughout his life, including bouts of severe Rheumatism - the general term of musculoskeletal disorders that cause intense chronic pain and inflammation in the body's array of connective tissues. A false rumour of his demise only served to exacerbate Garvey's health issues to the point that it seemingly played a big part in his death at the age of fifty-two. He had suffered a stroke in January 1940 while residing in London which had left him largely immobile, and his secretary, Daisy Whyte, subsequently became his full-time carer. George Padmore - a leading Pan-Africanist, journalist, and author who was a fierce rival of Garvey - intentionally spread untrue rumours that Garvey had died from the stroke to other journalists. This caused many national newspapers to publish premature obituaries in May 1940, and Garvey had the misfortune of reading some of these articles as he recovered from the stroke at a rented home in Kensington. According to Whyte's account of events, Garvey was busy reading through the newspapers that were falsely reporting on his death when he suffered another massive stroke. He died two weeks later on 10 June 1940 having never set foot in Africa. Numerous memorial services were held in honour of Garvey in the wake of his death, with large gatherings taking place in cities such as Kingston and New York City. Devoted followers of the political figure (called Garveyites) refused to believe that he had died, even when they were shown photographs of his body inside a coffin. They insisted that it was part of a conspiracy to undermine his movement. His body was originally interred in a vault located inside the chapel of St. Mary's Catholic Cemetery in Kensal Green, West London, until 1964 when it was then reburied in King George VI Memorial Park in Kingston. Garvey was posthumously pardoned by United States President Joe Biden in early 2025 in relation to Garvey being charged with mail fraud in 1922, for which he served part of a five-year prison sentence at the Atlanta Federal Penitentiary before he was deported from the United States to Jamaica in 1927.

President Biden acknowledged that the social activist had been mistreated after 102 years of injustice. A bronze statue of Garvey is located in his native town of St. Ann's Bay, Jamaica, and it was unveiled to recognise the importance of his pioneering political work.

The New York Times, 12th June 1940. "Harlem's 'Emperor of Africa,' who sold thousands idea of own nation, dies in London" Marcus Garvey: Look For Me in the Whirlwind. **TV Documentary (2001)**
Dayton Daily News, 6th February 2004. "Marcus Garvey Profile"
The Daily Telegraph, 26th January 2008. "The rise and fall of Marcus Garvey"
Afrikan Mind Reconnection & Spiritual Re-Awakening Volume I, **PP. 201-204. Dr. Lumumba Umunna Ubani (2011)**
The Spectator Magazine, 21st January 2025. "Joe Biden was right to pardon Marcus Garvey"

SOARING ABOVE

Thomas Francis Mantell Jr.

June 30th 1922 - January 7th 1948

On 7 January 1948, American National Guard Capt. Thomas Mantell Jr. died when his F-51 Mustang fighter jet crashed near Franklin, Kentucky, after he was ordered to pursue an unidentified flying object (UFO). Mantell and two other planes intercepted the object at an altitude of 15,000 feet over the town of Madisonville, after the local Kentucky State Police Department received a large number of calls regarding the UFO. Mantell said that he was chasing "a metallic object of tremendous size" during one of his last radio transmissions. He continued to climb to 22,000 feet without the other two pilots, who wisely chose not to follow him as the old World War II planes were not equipped with oxygen. They tried to contact Mantell via radio to request that he discontinue his ascent since his aircraft also lacked requisite oxygen equipment for high-altitude flight - they received no response. Officials from the United States Military later determined that Mantell had likely blacked out from a lack of oxygen once he reached 25,000 feet, and his plane began to plummet back towards the ground. He would become the first flight casualty of the Kentucky Air National Guard when his F-51 Mustang crash-landed in the front lawn of a farmhouse. The military initially gave contradicting explanations for the cause of the crash before they eventually announced to the press that Mantell had died "chasing Venus". Declassified documents obtained in 1952 reported that the object Mantell had been pursuing was a Skyhook balloon - a top-secret project that he would've had no knowledge about at that time. Skyhook balloons had the potential to reach an altitude of up to 100,000 feet, so it's assumed that Mantell lost consciousness whilst he chased one into the atmosphere without being equipped with oxygen. Not everyone agrees with this explanation however, including eyewitnesses on the day of the event. A man named Richard T. Miller claims that he was present in the Scott AFB operations room located in Belleville, Illinois, during Mantell's encounter with the object. He claims that the pilot's last words were: "My god, I see people in this thing!" Another man called James F. Duesler, a crash scene investigator who saw the wreckage of Mantell's plane, said that the captain's plane had landed flat on the ground - something which is highly unusual for an uncontrolled crash. Multiple theories have been put forward in the years since the event, with alien involvement being one of the most popular explanations proposed by conspiracy theorists. Mantell's remains were removed from the wreckage and buried in Zachary Taylor National Cemetery in Jefferson County, Kentucky. The Simpson County Historical Society unveiled a historical landmark in honour of Mantell just outside of his hometown of Franklin on 29 September 2001. The marker contains a brief account on Mantell's life and the odd circumstances surrounding his death.

The Baltimore Sun, 9th January 1948. "Pilot Dies Chasing 'Disk'; 'Red Cone' Seen in Ohio"

Detroit Free Press, 9th January 1948. "Pilot Dies Chasing Flying Disk"

The Albuquerque Journal, 21st August 1952. "Pilot's account of 'death flight' pursuing 'flying object' revealed"

Smokin' Rockets: The Romance of Technology in American Film, Radio and Television, 1945-1962, **PP. 19-20. Patrick Lucanio & Gary Coville (2002)**

Extraterrestrials and the American Zeitgeist: Alien Contact Tales Since the 1950s, **P. 37. Aaron John Gulyas (2013)**

AN UNFITTING END

MARGO JONES

DECEMBER 12th 1911 – JULY 24th 1955

Nicknamed the "Texas Tornado", Margo Jones was a renowned American stage director and producer from the small town of Livingston in Polk County, Texas. She is best known for kick-starting the American regional theatre movement when she established the first regional professional company in the United States in 1947. Her Theatre '47 complex in Dallas introduced the theatre-in-the-round concept to American audiences when it opened its door to spectators during the summer of 1947. The establishment would alter its name to the corresponding year each time a new year began, but it was often simply called "Margo's" by the majority of people. Jones had a knack for writing her own new material to perform on-stage, and it's estimated that around one-third of the newly crafted plays that she created continued to be re-enacted on stage, television, and local radio decades after she perished. Jones's catalogue of work helped to inspire a range of playwrights in the early stages of their careers, including prominent figures such as Tennessee Williams and Robert E. Lee. Williams himself said that Jones was a combination of Joan of Arc, Gene Autry, and nitroglycerine when he was asked to describe his idol. It's a great shame that Jones's dream of a decentralised American theatre was only just coming to fruition when she died on 24 July 1955. She had invited friends to a party at her residence a week prior to her death on 17 July, and at some point during the evening Jones accidentally spilled paint on an expensive carpet in one of the rooms of her house. She then contacted her personal secretary for advice, who in turn hired professional cleaners to deal with the issue. The cleaners quickly arrived and used carbon tetrachloride - a non-flammable chemical compound that was commonly used at the time - to remove the stains from the carpet. Jones was satisfied with the cleaning process, and she went to bed as normal later that night. However, she was unaware that some of the carbon tetrachloride had been absorbed into the carpet and eventually evaporated, filling her home with toxic fumes. Jones woke up the following morning feeling dizzy; the fumes had made her kidneys fail and she was extremely disorientated. She would be rushed to hospital later that afternoon after she was found unconscious on the sofa in her living room. Close friends who visited her in hospital claimed that Jones managed to briefly regain consciousness, and she was informed that she was going to die. She made elaborate preparations for her burial upon hearing this startling revelation, which included a request for her body to be dressed and groomed appropriately on the day of her funeral. Jones ultimately passed away at the age of forty-three after spending a few days in hospital. Her theatre dissolved four years after her death and was replaced by the Dallas Theatre Centre in late 1960. The area where the original complex stood is now occupied by the Nouveau 47 Theatre. The Margo Jones Award was established in 1961 in her honour, and it is awarded annually to an outstanding individual who has made significant contributions in the field of playwriting.

The New York Times, 4ᵗʰ June 1947. "STAGE FOLK STUDY THEATRE IN DALLAS; Margo Jones' New Company Attracting Wide Attention - Offers Several Premieres"

The Courier-Gazette, 25ᵗʰ July 1955. "Margo Jones, Play Producer, Dies In Dallas"

WBAP-TV (Television station: Fort Worth, Texas) **26th July 1955.**

UNT Digital Library - retrieved 15ᵗʰ January 2025.

A Marmac Guide to Dallas, **PP. 244-245. Yves Gerem (2004)**

Sweet Tornado: Margo Jones and the American Theater, **TV Documentary (2006)**

American Women Stage Directors of the Twentieth Century, **PP. 203-213. Anne Fliotsos & Wendy Vierow (2008)**

NEVER SAW IT COMING
ALAN STACEY
AUGUST 29th 1933 - JUNE 19th 1960

Alan Stacey's fatal crash is a striking example of just how random and unpredictable life can be at times, even with the best possible training and preparation. The British Formula One driver, aged twenty-six, crashed his vehicle and died during the Belgian Grand Prix on 19 June 1960. Reports suggest that a bird struck his helmet while he was driving at a high speed during the 25th lap of the race at the Circuit de Spa-Francorchamps, which caused Stacey to lose control of his Lotus 18-Climax. He crashed after the car climbed an embankment and went through ten feet of thick hedge at approximately 120 mph - the bird that hit him was killed instantly upon impact, according to eyewitnesses. He was violently thrown out of the vehicle when it landed in a nearby field. The Lotus immediately caught on fire, and Stacey was already dead by the time help arrived. He wasn't the only racer to die on the track that day, as fellow British racer Chris Birstow crashed his car and perished just a few minutes before Stacey during the 20th lap. Bristow's Cooper also hit an embankment and rolled over multiple times; he was decapitated when his body hurled through the air and struck a line of barbed wire. Aged only twenty-two when he died, Bristow was the youngest-ever driver to die in a Formula One World Championship event until twenty-year-old Ricardo Rodriguez died during a practice session for the Mexican Grand Prix in 1962.

The Scotsman, 20th June 1960. "Alan Stacey Stuck in Face by Bird"

The New York Times, 20th July 1960. "2 Rookie Drivers Die In Grand Prix; Stacey and Bristow Killed in Separate Crashes in Race Won by Brabham"

Cars At Speed: The Grand Prix Circuit, **P. 124. Robert Daley (1961)**

Motorsport Magazine, April 1997. "Chris Bristow & Alan Stacey: Two young to die"

Circus Before Dawn, **P. 480. David Miller (2010)**

DON'T SPEAK TOO SOON
JEROME IRVING RODALE
AUGUST 16th 1898 - JUNE 8th 1971

Jerome Irving Rodale, a pioneering figure in the organic farming movement and a staunch advocate for sustainable living, met a sudden end during the taping of an interview. His death became a poignant moment in the history of health and wellness, underscoring the complexities of human life and the unpredictability of fate. Rodale's work was revolutionary at a time when industrial agriculture was on the rise. He emphasised the importance of soil health, arguing that the quality of food was directly linked to the quality of the soil in which it was grown. His advocacy laid the groundwork for the modern organic food industry, and inspired generations of farmers, consumers, and environmentalists. His demise was as dramatic as it was ironic. He appeared as a guest on *The Dick Cavett Show* - a popular late-night talk show - to discuss his views regarding health and longevity on 8 June 1971. During the interview, Rodale famously declared: "I'm going to live to be 100, unless I'm run down by a sugar-crazed taxi driver." His confidence in his health and lifestyle was on display, as he had long promoted the benefits of organic living and natural health practices. However, shortly after making this bold statement, Rodale suffered a fatal heart attack and couldn't be revived. The episode was never aired to the public, and news of his death spread quickly. The irony of a health advocate dying from a heart attack during a TV interview whilst discussing the subject of longevity was not lost on the public. Critics of Rodale seized upon the incident; many of them used it as a reason to question the validity of his claims. His supporters argued that the heart attack he had suffered was not a reflection of his lifestyle, but rather a reminder of the limitations of human control over health. Rodale's legacy still endures, despite the circumstances surrounding his death. His work laid the foundation for the organic food industry, which has grown exponentially in the decades since his passing. The Rodale Institute - founded by his son Robert Rodale - continues to be a leading voice in organic farming research and education.

DID YOU KNOW?

The world of comedy lost one of its most unique and irreverent talents, Dick Shawn, on 17 April 1987 in a manner similar to how Rodale had died sixteen years prior. He was performing his one-man show, *The Second Greatest Entertainer in the Whole Wide World,* at the University of California, San Diego. He delivered a monologue about a heart attack during the performance, humorously describing the experience of collapsing during a live performance. Moments later, he suffered an actual heart attack and collapsed. The audience, believing it was part of the act, initially laughed and applauded - it was only when the show did not resume that they realised something was terribly wrong. Shawn was pronounced dead that night at the age of sixty-three. His sudden and unexpected death marked the end of an era for a man who had largely redefined the boundaries of stand-up comedy and theatrical performance.

The Washington Post, 9th June 1971. "Organic Food Pioneer Dies on TV Show"

Associated Press, 9th June 1971. Health publisher dies on TV show"

The Los Angeles Times, 18th April 1987. "Comedian Dick Shawn dies on stage in San Diego"

Fear and Loathing of Boca Raton: A Hippie's Guide to the Second Sixties, **P. 133. Steven Lewis (2007)**

The New York Times, 3rd May 2007. "When that guy died on my show"

The New Republic Magazine, 7th August 2014. "The Bizarre Life (and Death) of "Mr. Organic"

The Show Won't Go On: The Most Shocking, Bizarre, and Historic Death of Performers Onstage, **PP. 18-22. Jeff Abraham & Burt Kearns (2019)**

THE LAST SUPPER
BANDO MITSUGORO VIII
OCTOBER 19th 1906 - JANUARY 16th 1975

Kabuki is a form of dance drama that's immensely popular in Japan. One of its most revered practitioners was the legendary Bando Mitsugoro, a figure considered so important that the Japanese government awarded him the status of "living national treasure" in 1973. He would be dead just two years after receiving the prestigious title, when he knowingly consumed large amounts of poison on 16 January 1975 while in the company of his friends. Mitsugoro had certainly bitten off more than he could chew that evening at an elegant Kyoto restaurant, as the Kabuki actor convinced the head chef to serve him four portions of fugu kimo - better known as puffer fish liver. The sale of puffer fish liver was strictly prohibited by local ordinances (the ban would extend nationwide in 1984) and the chef was fully aware of the risks he was taking. Nonetheless, the chef granted Mitsugoro his wish, presumably because he didn't want to disrespect the actor in any way due to his high status among the Japanese populace. We can only hope that Mitsugoro enjoyed his meal: It was to be the last dish he would eat. Boasting to his friends in attendance that he could survive the toxic fish's poison, he ate the livers to prove his point. It turns out that he wasn't immune to the poison after all, for he began to develop severe symptoms shortly after the meal. He would ultimately die in his hotel room some seven hours later, with Mitsugoro experiencing gradual paralysis and breathing difficulties before he died. He was still able to communicate in the lead up to his death, and it's said that he openly admitted that he had been foolish to consume the deadly commodity - a case of too little, too late.

The Leader-Post, 20th January 1975. "Japanese Actor Poisoned"

The New York Times, 29th November 1981. "One Man's Fugu Is Another's Poison"

10 Ways to Recycle a Corpse: And 100 More Dreadfully Distasteful Lists, **P. 28. Karl Shaw (2011)**

Food History Almanac: Over 1,300 Years of World Culinary History, Culture, and Social Influence, **PP. 58-59. Janet Clarkson (2014)**

Japan Journal, 21st January 2022. "A dish to die for"

TOO MUCH TOO QUICKLY
PAULINE ANNIE SEWARD
DECEMBER 8th 1956 - AUGUST 23rd 1981

British model Pauline Seward periodically went on binges of starving and overeating to maintain her extremely slim figure. She had developed a crippling eating disorder due to her self-conscious nature, with the young model only consuming two large meals per week on average. Following a routine three-day fast, Seward decided to indulge in a huge meal that would bring about her death. The ill-fated midnight banquet consisted of two black puddings, two raw cauliflowers, one pound of liver, two pounds of peas, one pound of mushrooms, a large block of cheese, multiple pieces of bread and a large portion of various fruits. It's staggering that she managed to consume such a large quantity of food, especially considering the fact that she weighed under 40 kg. Her mother, Maureen Seward, stated that her daughter struggled to breathe and was suffering from abdominal pain when she discovered her not long after she had devoured the hefty meal. She was rushed to Royal Liverpool Hospital to undergo emergency surgery, but she sadly passed away following the unsuccessful procedure on 23 August 1981. It's reported that her stomach had enlarged and popped out, similar to what you would expect to see during pregnancy. Dr. Gordon Stampo - a leading coroner who carried out a post-mortem examination on Seward - said it was the first time that he had encountered such an unusual case, with Seaward's body simply unable to handle the large intake of food. Her death truly highlights the daily struggles that models have to contend with, as eating disorders are prevalent among young models who struggle to meet the industry's often unrealistic expectations.

The Liverpool Echo, 25th August 1981.

Coventry Evening Telegraph, 27th August 1981. "Young woman apparently ate herself to death"

The Straits Times, 29th August 1981. "Model who gorged herself to death"

Newcastle Evening Chronicle, 9th November 1981. "Model ate herself to death"

The Daily Mirror, 10th November 1981. "Killed Model"

The Forbidden Body: Why Being Fat is Not a Sin, **P. 62. Shelley Bovey (1994)**

DON'T FORGET YOUR GLASSES
REGINALD TUCKER
MARCH 7th 1955 - JULY 3rd 1984

Charismatic American lawyer Reginald "Reggie" Tucker really should've kept his glasses on; they might have preserved his life. The twenty-nine-year-old, who originally hailed from Detroit, was enjoying an early Independence Day party at the Schuyler Roche and Zwirner solicitors' firm located at the Prudential Building (now One Prudential Plaza) in Chicago on 3 July 1984 when he made a fatal error of judgement. Tucker was employed at the complex, and the gathering was attended by approximately fifty other employees of the law firm. The majority of the attendees had departed to go home by 11 pm, at which point Tucker and another male colleague decided to have an impromptu race in a corridor on the 39th floor of the building. For some unknown reason Tucker removed his shoes and spectacles in preparation for the race - a choice that would kill him. The competitors sprinted down the hallway as fast as they possibly could. It's unclear who won the race, but what is known is that Tucker careered straight through a window at the end of the corridor and fell over 800 feet to his death. It seems he had failed to realise that he was running directly into a large floor-to-ceiling window. Police officers said pieces of the lawyer's body were scattered around the street at the base of the tower. Downtown Chicago was flooded with partying civilians that night, so countless onlookers heard the loud shattering of glass and saw him plummet to his death.

Hundreds of people attending a lakefront fireworks show were also present in the area when the incident occurred. One horrified witness stated that it was "like an explosion" when Tucker's body smashed into a parked car. His contact lenses and glasses were later discovered on his office desk by other employees.

The Chicago Tribune, 5th July 1984. "Party horseplay proves fatal for lawyer in 39-floor plunge

The Journal Times (Wisconsin), 5th July 1984. "Lawyer Plunges to His Death"

Detroit Free Press, 6th July 1984. "A promising career, shocking end"

https://darwinawards.com/darwin/darwin1994-02.html

THE LAST SNIFF
COCAINE BEAR
DISCOVERED DECEMBER 22nd 1985

In the annals of bizarre real-life stories, few capture the imagination quite like the Cocaine Bear incident. The real-life tale took place in the dense forests of Georgia, United States, in September 1985, and it involves a female black bear, a convicted felon, and several duffel bags filled with cocaine. A former narcotics officer turned drug smuggler named Andrew Thornton II was piloting a small plane loaded with cocaine from Colombia to the United States on 11 September 1985 when something went horribly wrong as he flew over Georgia. Thornton - also a seasoned sky diver - and fellow smuggler, Bill Leonard, were both equipped with parachutes, and they decided to bail out of the plane when it became apparent that they were going to crash. Leonard survived the ordeal, but Thornton died as his parachute failed to open. The FBI said that the men had dropped around forty plastic containers full of cocaine into the wilderness before abandoning the plane in the skies above Knoxville, Tennessee. The cargo had been dumped because the combined weight of two men, in addition to the large quantity of cocaine, was too heavy for the small plane to carry. Thornton landed in a driveway in Knoxville, and investigators discovered that he had a duffle bag strapped to his body which contained cash, firearms, and approximately 35 kg (77 pounds) of cocaine. The plane, now pilotless, crashed in the Chattahoochee National Forest in northern

Georgia. The wreckage was eventually located by law enforcement, and they realised that there was a substantial amount of drugs missing from the plane. Unbeknownst to them, a black bear had stumbled upon some of the duffle bags filled with cocaine that had been jettisoned from the plane. The bear, curious and hungry, tore into the bag and consumed an enormous amount of the class A drug. It is unclear exactly how much cocaine the bear ingested, although it was definitely enough to kill it. Bears (like humans) are highly sensitive to stimulants, and the sheer quantity of cocaine ingested would have undoubtedly been fatal. The bear's body was found in late December 1985, surrounded by torn-open packages of cocaine. Chief medical examiner Dr. Kenneth Alonso stated that the bear's stomach was "literally packed to the brim with cocaine", and it earned the nicknames "Pablo Eskobear" and "Cocaine Bear". The story of the Cocaine Bear has taken on a life of its own in recent years. It has been the subject of numerous articles, podcasts, and even a book entitled *The Bluegrass Conspiracy* which delves into the broader context of drug smuggling in the American South during the 1980s. In 2023, the tale was adapted into a darkly comedic film titled Cocaine Bear, directed by Elizabeth Banks. The movie, while heavily fictionalized, introduced the bizarre story to a new generation. The bear itself was taxidermied and has been displayed in various locations, including a Kentucky mall and a restaurant. It remains a curious and darkly humorous symbol of the infamous 1980s drug culture.

Lexington Herald-Leader, 23rd December 1985. "Georgia bear found dead near cocaine shipment"

The New York Times, 23rd December 1985. "Cocaine and a dead bear"

Cocaine Bear: The True Story. **TV Documentary (2024)**

The Washington Post, 24th February 2023. "The strange true story behind Cocaine Bear and Andrew Thornton"

Entertainment Weekly Magazine, 28th September 2023. "The true story of Elizabeth Banks' Cocaine Bear explained"

RUNWAY RAMPAGE

DANIEL JOHN O'BRIEN

OCTOBER 31st 1958 – JANUARY 14th 1990

When David Meyer settled into his bed for the night at around 9:30 pm at the Bel Air International Airport Hotel in Piarco, Trinidad, on 14 January 1990, he couldn't possibly have anticipated being abruptly awoken half an hour later by his Daniel John O'Brien - who was completely naked - choking him with his bare hands. Flabbergasted as to why he was being attacked in his sleep, Meyer began to fight back and a struggle ensued between the men. O'Brien grabbed a bedside reading lamp and struck Meyer on the head with the object, knocking him out cold. The seemingly deranged O'Brien then ran straight out into the hotel corridor, where he picked up a twenty-pound fire extinguisher and attempted to spray the contents down his throat (he failed to do so) in front of bewildered onlookers. When this attempt failed, he dropped the fire extinguisher and ran out of the hotel. Once outside he climbed over a ten-foot wired fence that separated the hotel from the runways at Piarco International Airport and ran in the direction of a hanger located on the Northwest side of the compound. Airport security officers were immediately dispatched to apprehend him after they were notified that a trespasser had gained access to the runway. The officers managed to quickly subdue O'Brien before they placed him into the back of a jeep to be transported to the airport's security office. O'Brien somehow succeeded in overpowering the driver as they were travelling towards the main building of the airport, and he forced the other security officers out of the vehicle. Now in full control of the jeep, he jumped into the driver's seat and drove off down the runway. As these events were unfolding, British Airways flight 256 - destined for London via Barbados and Antigua - sat at the end of the runway awaiting clearance for take-off. O'Brien purposely crashed the jeep directly into the plane's underbelly after he spotted the aircraft sitting idly. The collison tore off the entire roof of the jeep and shattered the steering wheel. O'Brien miraculously emerged from the wreckage alive; although he had sustained visible wounds to both his chest and shoulder. Passengers aboard the British Airways flight witnessed him rubbing a combination of blood and leaking jet fuel all over his body, with eyewitnesses claiming that he "looked like a man who was possessed" as he limped around outside the plane. Then, without warning, O'Brien suddenly ran towards one of the plane's wings and threw himself inside a still-functioning jet engine. He was shredded into multiple pieces in an instant, with some of his remains being discovered over twenty feet away from the engine. A large portion of his upper body became wedged in the engine, causing it to malfunction. All passengers were ordered to disembark the aircraft as the captain informed them that the flight had been cancelled - it's reported that eleven other flights had to be delayed as a result of O'Brien's actions. Meyer was found unconscious by staff members at the Bel Air Hotel, and he was transported to a local hospital to receive treatment for the wounds he had sustained. A lingering question has always remained unanswered: What had caused O'Brien to react in such an absurd manner? Meyer claimed that his friend had become agitated shortly before the strange events took place because he was unable to find suitable medication for an undiagnosed health issue. The security guards who briefly apprehended O'Brien also said that he was shouting about how he had recently murdered his friend, so it's possible that he thought he had actually killed Meyer, which in turn could have made his erratic behaviour even worse. The true reason for his bizarre actions is never likely to be understood. Suicide is listed as the cause of death, and his body was swiftly returned to the United States to receive an appropriate burial.

The Times Leader from Wilkes-Barre, 16th January 1990.
"American tourist throws himself into jet engine"
The Trinidad Guardian, 16th January 1990. "Bizarre death at Piarco: Visitor minced to bits by jet engine"
Los Angeles Times, 17th January 1990. "American killed when he jumps into jet's engine"
The Chicago Tribune, 18th January 1990. "Man killed by a jet engine lacked medicine, friend says"
https://www.cracked.com/article_32029_7-horror-stories-that-came-from-real-life-not-movies.html

DEATH IN THE WILDERNESS
THE KHAMAR-DABAN INCIDENT
AUGUST 5th 1993

A group of Ukrainian kayakers had their idyllic trip in the Siberian wilderness completely shaken up when they stumbled across a hysterical teenage girl wandering alone by the shoreline on 9 August 1993. Her blood-curdling screams had attracted the group's attention, with the female's clothing completely soaked in blood. She continued to mumble incoherent words as she ran towards the startled kayakers, who were unaware of the fact that the delirious girl was the sole survivor of a gruesome tragedy that came to be known as the Khamar-Daban Incident. The group placed her into one of their kayaks and took her to the nearest police station where a report was filed. Police officers soon came to realise that she was seventeen-year-old Valentina Utochenko, a Kazakhstani national who had been a member of a hiking party in the Khamar-Daban mountain region. Utochenko refused to speak to anyone for almost two weeks, meaning the official search for her companions was not launched until 24 August. Helicopters searched the mountains for two days before the bodies of the six other hikers were located - rescue crews were only given a vague idea of where to search because Utochenko had been unable to recount her version of events, so they had to scour the entire area. The bodies of the deceased were noted to have been partially undressed when they were discovered, and further examinations revealed that all of them had died with horrified expressions etched across their faces. The six deceased Kazakhstani hikers were Aleksander Kyrsin, twenty-three; Tatyana Filipenko, twenty-four; Denis Shvachkin, nineteen; Viktoriya Zalesova, sixteen; Timur Bapanov, fifteen; and the group's leader Lyudmila Korovina, forty-one. They were said to have been a tight-knit bunch of good friends who always looked out for each other. Everyone in the group was physically fit, and they had all participated in difficult hikes prior to the fatal trip. Utochenko was finally able to speak to police officers shortly after the bodies were recovered, and she told a harrowing tale that shocked everyone involved in the investigation. The group of students visiting the Khamar-Daban mountains in the southern region of Siberia had set off on their arduous journey on 2 August. Their plan was to hike from the shores of Lake Baikal until they reached the summit at Kang-Ula, a distance of approximately 136 miles (220 km). Everything was going smoothly until 5 August, when Aleksander Kyrsin screamed out in agony as he was hiking behind everyone else at the back of the group. He was frothing from the mouth, and blood began to pour out from his eyes, ears, and nose before he fell to the ground unconscious. Korovina ran over to his location to help, but she also began to develop the same symptoms that Kyrsin had displayed. One by one each member of the group was struck down by the mysterious illness except for Utochenko, who was now all alone in the wilderness having just witnessed all of her friends perish in quick succession. She retreated down to the bottom of the mountain, where she set up a tent for the night and fell asleep. The realisation that she didn't have enough supplies to survive in the harsh conditions forced Utochenko to return to the site where her friends had died the following day to retrieve the items she required. She collected the leftover supplies and proceeded to wander for four days until she was rescued by the kayakers. The bodies of her friends underwent autopsies in Ulan-Ude after they were recovered to determine their causes of death. The autopsies revealed that all of the hikers had died due to hypothermia except for Korovina, as she had apparently succumbed to a heart attack. Protein deficiency - caused by malnutrition - was listed as a contributing factor in their deaths. Multiple theories have been proposed by leading experts to try and explain the cause of their sudden deaths, including the possibility that they died from altitude sickness or went mad because of infrasounds. The event has been likened to the infamous Dyatlov Pass Incident that took place in 1959, earning it the nickname "Buryatia's Dyatlov Pass". What really happened at the Khamar-Daban mountain range on that fateful day in August 1993 remains a mystery.

Lake Baikal and Its Life, **P. 7. M. Kozhov (2013)**
Russia Beyond Newspaper, 25th February 2019. "Beyond the Dyatlov mystery: 2 other creepy tragedies in the Russian mountains"
Thought Catalog Magazine, 7th December 2021. "The group of Russian hikers who started bleeding from their eyes"
The Khamar-Daban Incident - Weirder Than Dyatlov Pass? 13 O'Clock Podcast, **Ep. 383. Podcast (2023)**

The Khamar-Daban Incident: Mystery in the Mountains, Redhanded Podcast, **Ep. 355. Podcast (2024)**

THE HANDLESS SCREENWRITER
GARY MARTIN DEVORE
SEPTEMBER 17th 1941 - JUNE 28th 1997

Gary Martin DeVore was a well-respected screenwriter whose mysterious death continues to intrigue researchers and conspiracy theorists. The California native made a name for himself in Hollywood during the 1980s by writing a number of scintillating action scripts, including the 1986 blockbuster movie *Raw Deal* starring Arnold Schwarzenegger. DeVore was working on a new script entitled *The Big Steal* when he suddenly vanished in the early hours of 28 June 1997. He had been working tirelessly to finish the screenplay at his private office in Santa Fe - he chose to do much of his writing there as the change of scenery helped to cure his writer's block - until 1 am, at which point he finally decided to call it a night. He contacted his wife via a cellphone to inform her that he was about to drive home through the Mojave Desert. This was the last time that anybody heard from him, and a massive search was launched after he failed to return home. Extensive ground and air searches failed to find any trace of DeVore; a wanted poster, various newspaper articles, and an airing of a segment on "America's Most Wanted" tv show failed to provide any answers as to how he had disappeared. Over a year later, on 8 July 1998, a private investigator named Douglas Crawford discovered Devore's 1997 Ford Explorer submerged in water over an aqueduct in Palmdale, California. Devore's badly decomposed body was found in the driver's seat of the car, and investigators were unable to determine a cause of death as he had been submerged under water for a long period of time. The corpse wasn't fully intact either. His hands had been removed; human hand bones were found close to where the vehicle had been discovered, although they couldn't be conclusively identified as DeVore's. His death was ultimately ruled accidental, but the official explanation provided by members of the California Highway Patrol simply doesn't add up. They concluded that DeVore had driven in the wrong direction on the Antelope Valley Freeway until he eventually reached a freeway off-ramp. He then cleared an unfenced embankment whilst travelling at around 70 mph, which caused the car to crash into a deep body of water above the aquaduct. The location where DeVore was discovered had been searched multiple times prior to his body being located on 8 July 1998, meaning it could have been overlooked on previous occasions, or somebody placed both the vehicle and DeVore's body there at some point after the initial searches had been conducted. In addition, no motorists or pedestrians ever witnessed DeVore driving on the wrong side of the freeway - which he apparently did for a distance of three miles - against oncoming traffic. Another interesting point to note is that his laptop, which contained the only copy of *The Big Steal,* and personal firearm were both missing from his car after the police had pulled it out of the water. Unsurprisingly, the strangeness of the case caused a stir and resulted in a whole host of conspiracy theories, one of which blamed the CIA for DeVore's death. The case is still being actively investigated to date.

Entertainment Weekly Magazine, 1st August 1997. "The disappearance of Gary DeVore"

The Independent, 20th September 1997. "Hope fades for the vanished film writer"

The Los Angeles Times, 9th July 1998. "Missing writer's body believed found"

Santa Barbara Independent, 25th July 2010. "Autopsy Suggests Former Carp Screenwriter Was Murdered"

Bizarre Conspiracies: Hollywood's Lost Script - The Gary DeVore Mystery. **Podcast (2024)**

https://www.vice.com/en/article/the-writer-with-no-hands-gary-devore-matthew-alford/

TOXIC INTIMACY
MARIO BUGEANU & MIRELA IANCU
MARCH 21st 1999

Never get distracted from what's happening around you, even if you're engaging in sexual intercourse. Twenty-four-year-old Romanian professional footballer Mario Bugeanu and his girlfriend, twenty-three-year-old Mirela Iancu, died from carbon monoxide poisoning on 21 March 1999 in the garage of Bugeanu's home in Transylvania as the horny couple inexplicably forgot to switch off the engine of the car they was having sex inside of. Bugeanu had only lived in the Bistrita region of Transylvania for two months, having joined local Romanian First Division club Gloria Bistrita on loan from Rapid Bucharest during the 1999 January transfer window. He had found his first-team opportunities limited at Rapid since making his debut for the club during the 1996-97 season, therefore he was transferred to Gloria Bistrita on a short loan deal to gain some extra minutes on the field and prove his worth to the management team at Rapid. Bugeanu clearly had other things on his mind however. He and his girlfriend had arrived back at Bugeanu's house after spending a romantic evening together, and they were obviously in the mood to get it on - they didn't have the patience to wait until they entered the house, so they decided to get down-and-dirty in the garage once Bugeanu had parked the car. The couple became intoxicated by the gases that were omitting from the car's exhaust, and the engine was found to still be running the following morning when the player's father came across their naked bodies inside the car when he entered the garage. Fans of Rapid haven't forgotten Bugeanu in the years since his death, as many passionate supporters continue to light candles at his gravesite on the anniversary of his death each year to pay their respects.

The Iasi Newspaper, 23rd March 1999. "Mario Bugeanu has passed away".
Hurriyet Daily News, 24th March 1999. "Romanian player, girlfriend found dead".
The Miami New Times, 13th May 1999. "News of the Weird".
A Game of Three Halves: A Collection of Balls-Ups from the Beautiful Game, **P. 14. Charlie Croker (2002)**

ENRAGED BIRDS
WILFRED ROBY
1921/22 - JULY 5th 2002

Seagulls can be pesky little buggers at the best of times. These scavengers contrive to steal our food or defecate on us with annoying regularity, so it's best to keep your wits about you if you find yourself surrounded by lots of gulls. There are instances where they have caused physical harm to humans, even if they haven't been provoked in any way. This happened to an unlucky British retiree named Wilfred Roby; he got caught up in a bizarre incident involving a flock of seagulls that occurred on 3 July 2002, and it sadly ended with the death of the eighty-year-old. The former ambulance driver had been attempting to clear bird droppings from the roof of his garage in Anglesey, Wales, when he came across a nest full of chicks. Neighbours said that the nesting gulls then proceeded to attack Roby in large numbers, and he was forced to retreat from the roof. Not long afterwards, while standing in the front garden of his home, he suffered a severe heart attack and collapsed to the ground. Witnesses told of how the birds continued to attack neighbours whilst they tried in vain to revive the pensioner. Roby himself was also pecked at by some of the gulls as he fought for his life. Neighbour Brian Sowter said: "While we were there the gulls were still coming down and screeching and attacking us." Another resident who lived nearby, David Lewis-Roberts, claimed both he and his wife had been attacked by the birds on a number of occasions. Roby would sadly be pronounced dead shortly after paramedics arrived at his address.

BBC News, 5th July 2002. "The return of the seagulls"

The Liverpool Echo, 5th July 2002. "Gull attack horror"

The Independent, 30th June 2004. "Coming to a town near you… The birds"

Wordpress, 19th May 2015. "Has a seagull ever killed a human? - The Untweetable Truth"

HEADLESS RIDER

FRANCIS DANIEL "FRANKIE" BROHM
NOVEMBER 3rd 1981 - AUGUST 29th 2004

The death of twenty-two-year-old Louisville native Francis Daniel "Frankie" Brohm serves as a reminder of why you should never get behind the steering wheel of a car when you're drunk. Brohm and his friend, John Kemper Hutcherson, had been drinking heavily at a bar in County Georgia until the early hours of 29 August, and the duo only left to go home when Brohm said that he felt sick. The right thing to do was to call a taxi; but Hutcherson stupidly insisted on driving them both home, despite clearly being over the legal alcohol limit by that point. Brohm was overcome with an urge to vomit as they began the drive home, and he leaned his head out of the passenger seat window to relieve the symptoms of his inebriation. Hutcherson, struggling to maintain control of the vehicle in his intoxicated state, violently swerved off the road a short distance from the bar that they had been drinking in. The car then hit a telephone pole support wire that also struck Brohm as he was hanging his head out of the window, instantly decapitating him. In a bizarre twist, Hutcherson didn't seem to acknowledge the severity of the situation as he was so drunk, and he astonishingly reversed the car back onto the road before continuing his journey home. He drove twelve miles to his suburban Atlanta home alongside his headless passenger, with Brohm's blood splattered all over the inside of the car. Hutcherson parked the car in his driveway when he got home and went inside to sleep whilst still wearing his blood splattered clothes - Brohm's corpse remained undisturbed in the truck for hours. The body was discovered a few hours later by a shocked neighbour who was walking outside of his property in the company of his baby daughter. He swiftly notified authorities, and the police found Hutcherson asleep inside his bedroom, still wearing his bloody clothes and visibly inebriated. The police didn't suspect that foul play had occurred, with Hutcherson clearly remorseful for the role he had played in his friend's death. He received a five-year prison sentence in May 2005 after he pleaded guilty to vehicular homicide, as investigators believed his blood-alcohol level was more than twice the legal driving limit when the accident took place. Brohm's family had pleaded for leniency on Hutcherson's behalf, due to him being a childhood friend of the victim.

DID YOU KNOW?

Cases of mentally ill people living with the deceased bodies of their relatives for years after they die is not as rare as you may think. Death is inevitable, but some family members simply can't let go of a loved one that they've grown emotionally attached to over a long period of time. Middle-aged American male Robert James Kuefler of Minnesota lived with the bodies of his deceased mother and brother for an entire year after they both died of natural causes in 2015. The local police discovered the corpses after gaining entry to the family household in September 2016, with the overwhelming odour of decay leading them to the skeletal remains of Kuefler's mother in an upstairs bedroom and the body of his twin brother in the basement. Kuefler frequently told lies to ward off queries and visits from friends and other relatives, insisting that his mother and brother were both unwell. Police eventually charged him with interfering with a dead body or the scene of a death in October 2017. "What would you do?" he asked a reporter when questioned about why he didn't notify the authorities about the deaths sooner. There's also the case of elderly Irish woman Mary Ellen Lyons, who continued to sleep in the same bed alongside her sister Agnes's skeletal remains for months after she had died. Their brother Michael Lyons - nicknamed "Sonny" by his relatives - shared the bungalow with his two sisters, but he never knew that Agnes had passed away because his sisters were so reclusive. Agnes had been in poor health for a long time prior to her death, and it's speculated that she was bedridden. Sonny last saw Agnes over four years before she died, when she had returned home from a stint in hospital. He discovered his sister's remains on 4 August 2003 when he went to inform her that Mary Ellen had become ill, and he immediately contacted the police. The authorities decided not to press charges against either Mary Ellen or Sonny after conducting an investigation.

The Irish Examiner, 6th August 2003. "Body left rotting as brother and sister continued to live in house"

The Irish Times, 20th August 2003. "Woman lay dead for eight months in Mayo home"

The Courier-Journal, 1st September 2004. "Francis Brohn Obituary"

The Associated Press, 15th September 2004: "Driver in decapitation case released from jail"

Los Angeles Times, 26th May 2005. "5 Years for Driver in Ga. Decapitation"

The Washington Times, 7th October 2017. "Minnesota man lived with bodies of mom, brother for a year"

The independent, 10th October 2017. "Man lived with decomposing corpses of mother and twin brother for a year as he could not bear to report deaths"

Won Nothing Podcast: Francis Daniel Brohm Feat Where The Weird Ones Are Podcast. **EP. 37. Apple Podcast (2024)**

AN INCOMPREHENSIBLE SUICIDE
DAVID PHYALL
1958 - JULY 5th 2008

David Phyall was so "irrationally opposed" to leaving his repossessed home that he resorted to cutting off his own head with a chainsaw in a meticulously thought out manner. The block of flats where the fifty-year-old disabled British male resided was scheduled to be demolished, with Phyall being the last remaining resident to live within the building. Every single house except his was boarded up and completely empty. The local housing association (Atlantic Housing Ltd) made eleven offers of alternative accommodation in an attempt to try and convince Phyall to relocate, but he refused any and all proposals that were put forward. The matter had eventually gone to court to repossess the property, and the lone resident was ordered to leave his home in Bishopstoke, Hampshire, after being given an eviction notice. He still refused to budge; instead he decided to commit suicide in a way that he deemed fitting. A chainsaw was arranged in such a way that it would decapitate Phyall when it was activated, as he put a considerable amount of effort into planning the entire process that would facilitate his suicide. His elderly parents alerted the police when they could not contact their son at his flat on 5 July 2008. Police officers forced their way into the property and asked the parents to wait outside while they inspected the flat. The scene inside was gruesome - they found Phyall's headless corpse in the lounge underneath a snooker table, with blood splattering the walls, floor, and numerous items of furniture. His severed head was located next to the chainsaw on the floor nearby. Recording a verdict of suicide, coroner Simon Burge said: "I think he did it to draw attention to the injustice of his situation."

The Southern Daily Echo, 14th July 2008. "Man found with head severed by chainsaw"

The Sydney Morning Herald, 20th November 2008. "UK man kills himself with chainsaw"

10 Ways to Recycle a Corpse: And 100 More Dreadfully Distasteful Lists, **P. 303. Karl Shaw (2011)**

Supernatural: 300 Horror Stories, Mysteries and Urban Legends, **P. 41. Cael Novak (2019)**

SUBMERGED IN CHOCOLATE
VINCENT JAMES SMITH II
DECEMBER 7th 1979 - JULY 8th 2009

Vincent James Smith II died just two weeks after starting his new role of employment at a poorly maintained chocolate-making factory located in Camden, New Jersey on 8 July 2009. Management at the facility regularly failed to implement safeguarding measures designed to protect staff, partly due to the fact that the facility hadn't been inspected for many months at the time of Smith's death. He was standing on a platform feeding huge chunks of raw chocolate into an eight-foot deep vat when he suddenly fell through an unguarded opening in the walkway and plunged directly into the vat, which was mixing and melting chocolate at scorching temperatures. It's reported that Smith had lost his footing after he slipped on the wet chocolate that had leaked onto the area where he was standing, and there were no protective railings in place to prevent workers from tumbling off the narrow walkway. The twenty-nine-year-old was fatally struck by a mixing blade that was attached to a rotating paddle inside the tank, causing his body to twist and contort into all kinds of unnatural positions. Smith's co-worker attempted to save him, but it was to no avail as the shut-off switch was located far away from the platform. His body remained stuck in the boiling chocolate - said to be at a temperature of around 120 degrees - for over ten minutes until emergency personnel managed to pull him out. Firefighters at the scene were almost entirely covered head-to-

toe in chocolate, as was the co-worker who tried to save Smith's life. Federal authorities subsequently fined the plant - owned by Cocoa Services Inc - $39,000 for several safety violations, including the absence of warning signs and guard rails.

The Associated Press, 8th July 2009. "Man Dies After Falling Into Tank of Chocolate"

The Daily Telegraph, 9th July 2009. "Man dies after falling into vat of chocolate"

Wordpress: "Death By Chocolate", **9th July 2009.**

https://www.nj.com/news/2009/07/facility_where_worker_fell_int.html

DON'T MAKE WAVES
ANTHONY SCOTT HENSLEY
SEPTEMBER 14th 1974 – APRIL 14th 2012

An American caretaker named Anthony Hensley, who worked for a company called Knox Swan & Dog that specialises in providing swans to clients who wish to scare off geese, drowned after a disgruntled swan attacked him and knocked him out of his kayak in a residential pond in Des Plaines, Illinois. Hensley, aged thirty-seven, tried to swim to shore, but eyewitnesses told investigators from the local sheriff's office that a large number of swans continued to attack him and prevented him from surfacing - the caretaker wasn't wearing a life jacket at the time of the incident. A member of the public called emergency services to get help for the stricken caretaker. Dive teams managed to pull the father-of-two from the water around thirty minutes later, although he was already dead by then. An autopsy was performed on his body at the Advocate Lutheran General Hospital in Park Ridge, and it was confirmed that he had died from drowning. Investigators believe Hensley had encroached on the swan's territory, prompting the relentless attack that followed. "I find myself still scratching my head," said Cook County Sheriff Tom Dart. "This truly is one of the ones that keeps you from saying 'I've seen everything now.'" A local resident who watched the incident unfold stated that Hensley had actually been attempting to steal swan eggs from a nest in the pond when the mother swan charged at him to defend its offspring. His wife, Amy Hensley, filed two separate wrongful death lawsuits - one in 2012 and another in 2017 - after her husband drowned, seeking at least $50,000 in damages against the owners of the residential complex in Des Plaines, as she solely blamed them for the events that had transpired. The first lawsuit was dismissed in court, but there is little information available on the outcome of the second hearing, and there hasn't been any updates provided about the second lawsuit since it took place in late 2017.

The Los Angeles Times, 16th April 2012. "Killer swan attacks Illinois caretaker until he drowns"
BBC News, 17th April 2012. "Who, What, Why: How dangerous are swans?"
San Diego Union-Tribune, 17th April 2012. "Swan linked to suburban Chicago man's drowning"
Inside Edition, 22nd April 2012. "Man Killed In Swan Attack"
Chicago Daily Herald, 27th November 2012. "OSHA: No violations in man's swan-related drowning"
The Chicago Tribune, 7th December 2017. "Wife of man killed in 2012 Des Plaines swan attack files lawsuit"

A CRUEL TWIST OF FATE
HEVEL YILDIRIM
2000/01 - JULY 3rd 2014

"I am devastated, but what more can I say? In fact there is nothing at all to say. Even the prosecutor has said this incident could be the first of its kind around the world." These were the words of heartbroken Turkish man Mehmet Yildirim after his thirteen-year-old son Hevel was killed by a goat that he had acquired from a local market. Mehmet had purchased the goat on 3 July 2014 so he could use it as a sacrifice in celebration of the upcoming Muslim feast of Eid al-Adha - the feast honours the prophet Abraham's willingness to sacrifice his chosen son as an act of submission to God, and the sacrifice of animals is considered to be an integral part of the festival proceedings. There wasn't enough space to fit the goat inside the family's small apartment however, so Mehmet opted to store it on the roof of the building instead. The animal became aggressive once they gained access to the roof, and it tried to escape by jumping over a protective fence that surrounded the entire rooftop. The sacrificial goat then fell six floors and landed on Hevel, who was playing with a group of friends just outside of the apartment building. The critically injured boy was rushed to a hospital in Diyarbakir, but he could not be saved - the goat died immediately after it struck Hevel. The police launched an investigation into the incident, with one law enforcement officer calling the case "unprecedented." Hevel's death was eventually ruled to be accidental, and no further legal action was taken against Mehmet as he was cleared of any wrongdoing.

Hurriyet Daily News, 6th July 2014. "13-year-old killed after goat falls from roof of building in Turkey"

The Independent, 7th July 2014. "Thirteen-year-old boy killed in Turkey after sacrificial goat falls on him from six floor apartment building"

Metro News, 7th October 2014. "Boy killed by sacrificial goat which fell from roof"

The Weirdest Death: Retrograde. **Episode 53. Amazon Podcast (2021)**

BEYOND ONE'S CONTROL
JI'AIRE DONNELL LEE
AUGUST 22nd 2011 - MAY 22nd 2015

Losing a child is surely the most intensely painful experience that a parent can ever go through. It's therefore all the more difficult to imagine that incomprehensible pain that Romechia Simms must feel, as her actions resulted in the death of her three-year-old son Ji'Aire Donnell Lee. Simms - then aged twenty-four - never meant to harm her child intentionally; she had previously been diagnosed with schizophrenia, and was experiencing episodes of psychosis for a long period of time leading up to her son's death. According to the Charles County Sheriff's Office, Simms placed Ji'Aire on a swing in Wills Memorial Park located in LaPlata, Maryland, on the morning of 20 May 2015. She was suffering from a schizophrenic episode at the time, and wasn't in control of what she was doing. Simms then pushed Ji'Aire on the swing for almost two days straight - totalling around forty consecutive hours, with no members of the public intervening to help the toddler or checking to see if everything was okay. Simms continued to slowly push her son on the swing - who was likely pleading for his mother to stop - until he tragically passed away due to a combination of dehydration and hypothermia. A concerned civilian who lived close to Wills Memorial Park alerted the police after she witnessed Simms pushing her deceased son in the swing during a rain storm on 22 May 2015. Emergency services soon arrived at the scene, and Simms was arrested by the police. She told investigators that she had failed to take her medication for the previous two days, which can cause a return of previous psychosis. Simms was facing a prison sentence amounting to almost fifty years for a variety of charges, including manslaughter and child neglect resulting in a death. A judge would ultimately rule that Simms was not criminally responsible for her actions at a court hearing in February 2016. Her public defender had argued that Simms was thwarted in her attempts to get her son out of the swing by voices she was hearing from within her mind. The voices kept reassuring her that someone would come and take Ji'Aire out of the swing if she waited a little longer. Simms would be set free from the court on a five-year conditional release order, which included a stipulation that required her to undertake regular blood tests to prove that she was taking her medication. The lasting psychological damage of losing her son had taken a toll on Simms; she expressed deep remorse about Ji'Aire's death, and she said that she began to take therapy sessions twice a week to help her cope with the everlasting sense of guilt that she feels. There have been no updates on the whereabouts of Romechia Simms in recent times; it can only be hoped that her mental health has continued to improve on her road to recovery.

Cosmopolitan Magazine, 6th June 2015. "More Information Emerges About the Mother Found Pushing Dead Son in Swing"
The Sydney Morning Herald, 1st July 2015. "US boy found on swing died of hypothermia and dehydration, autopsy finds"

The Seattle Times, 22nd February 2016. "Plea deal means mom avoids jail in son's swing death"

The Washington Post, 22nd April 2016. "She was found pushing her dead son on a swing. Now she lives with what she lost"

Mental Health General, 15th February 2023. "Romechia Simms: Lives Destroyed"

https://jiairesworkgroup.org/

A CASE OF GROSS NEGLIGENCE
ATEEF RAFIQ
c. 1993 - MARCH 16th 2018

Ateef Rafiq went to the Star City cinema complex in Birmingham, United Kingdom, with his wife on 9 March 2018 for what was supposed to be a pleasant romantic encounter, but it would instead turn into a nightmarish scenario for the young couple. Rafiq accidentally dropped his mobile phone and keys under his reclining seat as the movie they were watching concluded, and he decided to go underneath the seat to retrieve his personal items. A huge problem arose while he was trying to find the items, as the motorised footrest began to lower onto Rafiq until he was pinned and unable to move - approximately 749 kg of pressure was applied to the back of his neck. His wife, Ayesha Sardar, rushed to get help, and staff battled for over fifteen minutes in a desperate bid to free him. Cinema workers eventually managed to remove bolts from the chair which allowed them to drag Rafiq's motionless body out from beneath the chair. He had unfortunately suffered a heart attack that was triggered by a lack of oxygen to the brain, and the father-of-one died a week later while in the intensive care unit at Heartlands Hospital. It turns out that the motor in the seat which Rafiq had chosen to sit in had blown a fuse, with the customised seat also missing a vital bar that could have released him manually when he became trapped. London-based cinema chain Vue Entertainment Ltd were fined £750,000 at Birmingham Crown Court in July 2021 for various health and safety breaches at its Star City venue in connection to Rafiq's death. The company pleaded guilty to two charges in court, one of which was failing to ensure that customers were not exposed to unnecessary risks, and the other related to the negligence the company displayed by not having any kind of suitable and sufficient risk assessment take place at the Star City venue at any point in time between January 2007 and March 2018. Representatives of Vue Cinemas subsequently apologised to the family of Rafiq at the court hearing, and all recliners of the type involved in the tragedy were removed after an internal review of the incident was conducted. Judge Heidi Kubik QC ordered Vue Entertainment Ltd to pay an additional £130,000 in costs, and she stated that Rafiq died in "an accident that never should have happened".

DID YOU KNOW?

A middle-aged Spanish woman, named in local media outlets as Concha M. N, was found deceased in an "unfrequented" area of the ABC Park Cinema located in Valencia, on Spain's east coast region, on 19 April 2016 after her body had remained there undiscovered for a whole week. A representative of the regional Valencian government, Juan Carlos Moragues, said it's likely that the woman passed out and fell down a flight of stairs when she entered an emergency exit after watching a movie seven days prior on 12 April. Her body was discovered by a cleaner between two sets of emergency doors at the bottom of some stairs in an underground area of the cinema. The female cleaner noticed a "strong smell" in the vicinity, and when she opened the emergency door she found the woman's body, which was already in an advanced stage of decomposition. There were splotches of blood covering the stairs and floor, adding further weight to the theory that she tripped or fell down the stairs. Personal items such as a bag and a pair of glasses were scattered on the floor next to the body. The woman had been reported missing by her husband on 13 April when she had failed to return home the evening prior. It is thought she may have tried to leave the cinema in a hurry after feeling unwell, and thereafter she wandered into the out of bounds area by accident.

The Local Espana, 21st April 2016.
The Daily Mirror, 21st March 2018. "Young dad who died in freak cinema seat accident named as witness tells how his poor wife was screaming his name"
The Coventry Telegraph, 16th May 2019. "Cinema customer died after becoming trapped under chair, inquest hears"
London Evening Standard, 20th July 2021. "Vue Entertainment fined £750,000 over cinema seat death"
Variety Magazine, 20th July 2021. "European cinema giant Vue fined $1 million for death of UK film-goer in 2018"
Business Matters Magazine, 21st July 2021. "Vue cinemas fined £750,000 over death of customer trapped by chair"

TOO HOT TO HANDLE
DARREN HICKEY
JULY 8th 1967 - APRIL 5th 2019

A British man died in the United Kingdom after he sampled a fishcake that was so hot it burnt his throat and caused him to stop breathing just hours later. Wedding planner Darren Hickey, aged fifty-one, was asked to try the small piece of fishcake by one of the chefs at a wedding venue he managed in Chorley, Lancashire, on 4 April 2019. His voice box began to swell almost immediately after he consumed it, and Hickey had to take himself to the urgent care ward at Chorley Hospital as the pain grew worse throughout the afternoon. The doctors at the hospital failed to adequately investigate or treat the issue; they only prescribed painkillers and told Hickey to return if the pain worsened - partly because of the rarity of the injury he had sustained, and the lack of visible burns to his mouth and tongue gave the doctors the false impression that it wasn't a serious health issue. It later transpired that the hospital didn't have the correct specialist equipment to detect the damage as it occurred deep within the pharynx. Hickey departed from the hospital to make his way home, but the swelling in his throat continued to intensify to the point that he had difficulty swallowing, and his breathing became more laboured. Niel Parkinson, Hickey's partner, discovered him choking in the bedroom of their house around 9 pm - about nine hours after he had eaten the fishcake - and quickly dialed 999 to request an ambulance. Paramedics attempted to stabilise Hickey at the scene before they rushed him to Royal Bolton Hospital, where he was pronounced dead in the early hours of 5 April 2019. An inquest into his death took place in October 2019, and senior coroner Alan Walsh recorded a verdict of accidental death.

The Bolton News, 9th October 2019. "Popular venue manager died in freak accident after burning his throat on hot fishcake"

Lancashire Evening Post, 10th October 2019. "Chorley Hotel manager Darren Hickey dies after eating fishcake"

The Daily Telegraph, 10th October 2019. "Wedding planner died after burning his throat on a hot fishcake"

The Independent, 10th October 2019. "Man died after eating fish cake so hot it left him unable to breathe"

Manchester Evening News, 27th November 2019. "Wedding venue whose manager died from eating hot fishcake reduces its opening hours"

https://historyandthings.com/2024/05/10/15-wierd-causes-of-death-you-cant-possibly-imagine/

WALKING ON THIN ICE
YURI ALFEROV, VALENTIN DIDENKO & NATALIA MONAKOVA
FEBRUARY 28th 2020

It's highly important not to become so immersed in the virtual world that you lose your sense of reality and make poor, life-threatening decisions. As humans we yearn for attention, and social media provides us with a platform to gain that sought after attention from others all across the globe. This isn't always necessarily a good thing though, as some popular social media personalities will put themselves into dangerous situations just to gain more popularity or show off their luxurious lifestyle online. Russian mother-of-two Ekaterina Didenko is a popular Instagram influencer who has amassed a substantial amount of followers on the platform by promoting healthcare products and giving advice on issues that people encounter on a daily basis. Her husband, thirty-two-year-old IT specialist Valentin Didenko, planned to surprise Ekaterina for her 29th birthday by throwing an expensive party at a pool complex in Moscow on 28 February 2020. Ekaterina recorded the event to share with her followers on Instagram, and she would unintentionally broadcast the death of her husband and two other friends that day after her birthday celebrations turned into a desperate fight for survival. Valentin decided to empty a 25 kg bag of dry ice into a sauna pool at her party to create a dramatic steam show for the special occasion - an unwise choice in such a poorly ventilated area. Dry ice is a solid form of carbon dioxide that can be lethal if dangerous amounts of the gas are inhaled within a confined space. All those who were present in the sauna room began to choke almost immediately, and several attendees lost consciousness after they had chosen to jump into the pool. Partygoers Natalia Monakova and Yuri Alferov, both aged twenty-five, were pronounced dead at the scene by paramedics after they failed to get out of the pool in time. Valentin would die later that day after being transferred to a local hospital in Moscow - all three of those that perished had died from acute carbon dioxide poisoning. Ekaterina - who is also a fully qualified pharmacist - and her friends who survived the tragic event were discharged from hospital after they received extensive treatment for carbon dioxide poisoning and severe chemical burns. The Russian Investigative Committee opened a criminal case against Ekaterina shortly after the incident occurred, citing death by negligence. There's no reliable information available to suggest that she has been criminally prosecuted since however, as the public figure continues to maintain a large amount of social media followers and still promotes medical related products for multiple companies across a variety of platforms.

The Moscow Times, 29th February 2020. "Three die at Moscow party after dry ice thrown into pool"

Business Insider Magazine, 1ˢᵗ March 2020. "3 people died at an Instagram influencer's birthday party in Moscow after dry ice was poured into a swimming pool"

The Straits Times, 1ˢᵗ March 2020. "Three die after dry ice stunt at Russian Instagram star's pool party goes awry"

International Business Times, 2ⁿᵈ March 2020. "How does dry ice kill? 3 dead at Instagram influencer's birthday party as special effects go awry"

The New York Post, 3ʳᵈ March 2020. "Russian Instagram influencer's birthday party leaves 3 dead after dry ice incident"

The Eastern Herald, 17ᵗʰ April 2023. "An influencer hosts a death birthday party - guests cheerfully jumped in the pool and choked"

DIED WHILE SERVING
CHRISTIAN BOLOK
1981/82 - OCTOBER 26th 2020

A Filipino police lieutenant was killed in the line of duty by a knife-wielding rooster during a raid to shut down a cockfight on 26 October 2020 in the province of Northern Samar, Philippines. There is a long history of legal (and illegal) cockfighting in the Philippines, but the sport was temporarily banned in the country in August 2020 after it was found to have been a source of Covid-19 infections throughout many provinces. Some citizens chose to disregard lockdown rules and host the events in secluded areas to avoid detection. Christian Bolok and several other police officers conducted a raid on a property in Madugang village after they had received an anonymous tip-off about an apparent mass gathering that was taking place. A commotion ensued once the police gained entry as a large number of spectators attempted to flee. Three male farmers were quickly arrested at the location for violating lockdown rules. Bolok, aged thirty-eight, then attempted to pick up one of the roosters that was used for cockfighting once tensions at the location had eased, but he failed to notice that it still had its gaff - a metal razor blade used to kill opponents in cockfighting - attached to one of its legs. The gaff slashed him across his left leg and severed his femoral artery; he bled to death in a matter of minutes in front of his colleagues. Provincial Governor Edwin Ongchuan claimed that the blade may have also been laced with poison by someone at the property, although this was never proven to be factually true. Bolok was a thirteen-year veteran of the force and had fathered three children. A total of seven fighting cocks - including the one that had inadvertently killed Bolok - were confiscated during the raid, and approximately 550 pesos (£7.50) in cash was also seized from the property.

Philippine News Agency, 16th October 2020. "Cops to keep a tight watch vs illegal cockfighting"

The Daily Star (Philippines), 27th October 2020. "Fighting cock kills police chief in Philippine raid"

South China Morning Post, 28th October 2020. "Philippine policeman killed by rooster during raid on illegal cockfight"

Complex Magazine, 28th October 2020. "Police officer killed by rooster while trying to break up cockfight in the Philippines"

The New Zealand Herald, 29th October 2020. "Police officer killed by rooster at illegal cockfight in the Philippines"

The New York Times, 29th October 2020. "Rooster kills police officer in Covid-19 lockdown raid"

IMMORTAL NO MORE
AMY CARLSON
NOVEMBER 30th 1975 - APRIL 20th 2021

The passing of Amy Carlson, a controversial religious leader and founder of the Love Has Won cult, marked the end of a tumultuous chapter in the world of spiritual movements. Carlson claimed to be a divine entity and the embodiment of "Mother God", and she presented herself as a beacon of hope in a world she described as corrupt and broken. Her journey as a spiritual leader began in the late 2000s when she founded Love Has Won - a movement that blended New Age spirituality, conspiracy theories, and Carlson's own claims of divinity. Her teachings, often disseminated through social media platforms such as YouTube and Facebook, attracted a small but dedicated group of followers who believed in her message of love, unity, and spiritual awakening. While Carlson's followers viewed her as a goddess, critics and outsiders raised alarms about the cult-like dynamics of Love Has Won. Reports emerged of Carlson's erratic behaviour, including claims of alcohol abuse and manipulative tactics to control her followers. Former members described an environment of isolation, financial exploitation, and psychological manipulation. Carlson's demands for absolute loyalty created a power dynamic in her group that left little room for dissent or critical thinking. Her death in April 2021 proved to be a stark and sobering moment for the vast majority of her followers. Carlson's body was discovered on 28 April 2021 at a mountain lodge in

Colorado, where she had been living with members of her movement. The odd circumstances of her death raised questions about the group's practices and showed just how far her followers were willing to go to uphold her teachings. Reports indicated that her body had been preserved with glitter and Christmas lights, a surreal and tragic reflection of the group's devotion to her. Police officers said that both of Carlson's eyes were missing, and her remains were mummified; its state of decay suggested that she had been dead for at least a couple of weeks. It was also reported that she only weighed around 34 kg at the time she passed away. Several members of Love Has Won were charged with abuse of a corpse and child abuse - due to the presence of two young children at the property. The charges highlighted the extreme and troubling dynamics within the group. Some of her most loyal followers refused to acknowledge her death, as they believed she was immortal and that her physical form was merely a vessel for her divine essence. An autopsy report released in December 2021 stated that Carlson had died from "global decline in the setting of alcohol abuse, anorexia, and chronic colloidal silver ingestion". She had been ingesting large amounts of colloidal silver, which can lead to seizures and organ failure if it's consumed over a long period of time. Carlson had told her followers that she had cancer in the later months of 2020, but an autopsy on her body found no trace of cancer. Love Has Won no longer operates under its original name, although some dedicated followers of Carlson continue to operate under new names or as members of offshoot groups.

The New York Times, 5th May 2021. "7 Arrested After Police Find Mummified Body in Colorado Home"

The Denver Post, 29th July 2021. "How did Love Has Won cult leader die? Coroner hopes to learn by testing body for heavy metals"

Business Insider Magazine, 14th August 2021. "Abuse, exploitation, and a mummified leader: Inside the bizarre cult Love Has Won"

Rolling Stone Magazine, 26th November 2021. "From 'Mother God' to Mummified Corpse: Inside the fringe spiritual sect Love Has Won"

Variety Magazine, 8th December 2023. "'Love Has Won: The Cult of Mother God' Director Answers Burning Questions: Why She Didn't Emphasize QAnon Propaganda - and How She Incorporated Amy Carlson's Corpse"

WRONG PLACE, WRONG TIME
SHIVDAYAL SHARMA
1940/41 - APRIL 18th 2023

An eighty-two-year-old pensioner from India was killed on 18 April 2023 when he was struck by a 1,000 pound cow that was thrown over 100 feet into the air after it was hit by an express train. The incident occurred while Shivdayal Sharma was preoccupied with relieving himself next to a section of railway track in the city of Alwar within the northern state of Rajasthan. It's reported that the animal was walking along the track close to Sharma when the express train came into view, and the locomotive didn't have sufficient time to slow down before it struck the cow head-on. The animal was catapulted into the air by the impact before it came back down towards ground level in the direction of where Sharma was standing. The former railway employee was hit by a portion of the cow's body and died on the spot. A friend of Sharma - who was also relieving himself not far away - narrowly avoided being hit by the large flying animal, and he quickly rushed to a nearby police station to inform them of what had happened. Sharma's body underwent a post-mortem examination shortly after his death, and it was confirmed that the old man had died from the serious internal injuries that he sustained when the cow struck him. His death prompted government officials to demand for improved regulation on the high-speed train route, as data suggests incidents involving cows intruding on train tracks is not a rare occurrence in that particular region of India. Indian Railways minister Ashwini Vaishnaw announced that new safety measures were going to be put in place in the aftermath of Sharma's death, such as removing litter and overgrown vegetation to prevent cows from staying in the areas near the railway tracks.

India Today Magazine, 20th April 2023. "Rajasthan: Cow, hit by Vande Bharat train, falls on man peeing on tracks, kills him"

The Daily Star, 21st April 2023. "Man urinating on train tracks is struck and killed by flying cow hit by train"

Free Press Journal, 21st April 2023. "Rajasthan: Vande Bharat hits cow that lands on man peeing on track in Alwar, both die"

The Western Standard, 24th April 2023. "Man killed by flying cow while urinating by railway tracks"

The Straits Times, 22nd November 2024. "Indian man urinating on train track dies after being hit by flying cow"

FAMOUS LAST WORDS

These last words range from profound to absurd, but they all provide a fascinating glimpse into the personalities and final moments of these famous individuals.

Benjamin Franklin (1706–1790)
When his daughter urged him to change his position so that he could breathe more easily, he merely replied: "A dying man can do nothing easy."

James French (1930–1966)
A convicted murderer, his last words before his execution by electric chair were: "How about this for a headline for tomorrow's paper? 'French Fries!'"
It's safe to say that this remark shocked everyone in attendance.

Voltaire (French philosopher, 1694–1778):
When asked to renounce Satan on his deathbed, he replied:
"Now is not the time to make new enemies."
A witty and sharp retort until the very end.

H.G. Wells (author, 1866–1946):
He told those around him:
"Go away. I'm all right."

A simple and dismissive final statement from the iconic science fiction writer.

John Sedgwick (Union general, 1813–1864):
During the Battle of Spotsylvania Court House, he ironically said:
"They couldn't hit an elephant at this distance."
Moments later, he was fatally shot by a Confederate sniper.

Emily Dickinson (poet, 1830–1886):
Her final statement was:
"I must go in, the fog is rising."
A poetic and enigmatic statement from one of America's greatest ever poets.

Marie Antoinette (Queen of France, 1755–1793):
After accidentally stepping on her executioner's foot, she reportedly said:
"Pardon me, sir, I did not mean to do it."
Her final words were overly polite, even in the face of death.

Pancho Villa (Mexican Revolutionary, 1878–1923):
His last words were said to be:
"Don't let it end like this. Tell them I said something."
A fittingly dramatic statement from a pivotal revolutionary.

Dominique Bouhours (French grammarian, 1628–1702):

A man obsessed with language, his last words were:

"I am about to—or I am going to—die; either expression is correct."

A true grammarian until his final breath.

Leonardo da Vinci (Italian polymath, 1452–1519):

His final phrase was:

"I have offended God and mankind because my work did not reach the quality it should have."

A humble statement from one of history's greatest artists, showing that he believed he should have achieved more in spite of his legendary status.

John Barrymore (actor, 1882–1942):

He apparently said:

"Die? I should say not, dear fellow. No Barrymore would allow such a conventional thing to happen to him."

A defiant and theatrical exit indeed.

Groucho Marx (comedian, 1890–1977):

On his deathbed, he reportedly said the following phrase:

"This is no way to live!"

Even in his final moments, he couldn't resist making a joke out of the situation.

Thomas Edison (inventor, 1847–1931):

His last words:

"It is very beautiful over there."

A mysterious and poetic statement about what lies beyond this world.

Winston Churchill (British Prime Minister, 1874–1965):
The inspirational British politician famously muttered:
"I'm bored with it all."
A surprisingly blunt and weary final statement from the iconic leader.

Lou Costello (comedian, 1906–1959):
His last words were:
"That was the best ice cream soda I ever tasted."
A lighthearted and unexpected final statement.

George Bernard Shaw (playwright, 1856–1950):
The renowned playwright famously said:
"Dying is easy; comedy is hard."
A witty and fitting remark from one of the greatest playwrights.

Hank Williams (musician, 1923–1953):
His last words, spoken to a chauffeur, were:
"We're going to the next town, and I'm gonna sing 'I'll Never Get Out of This World
Alive.'"
Ironically, he died in the backseat of the car before it could reach the next town.

Gustav Mahler (composer, 1860–1911):

The last thing he ever said was:

"Mozart! Mozart!"

A fitting tribute to the composer that he had admired so much.

Nostradamus (astrologer, 1503–1566):

His last words were:

"Tomorrow, I shall no longer be here."

A prophetic statement from the man known for his many predictions.

Frank Sinatra (singer, 1915–1998):

He was quoted as saying:

"I'm losing it."

A poignant and vulnerable final remark from the legendary crooner as he knew that his time had come.

William Palmer (convicted murderer, 1824–1856):

While standing on the gallows waiting to be executed, the unhinged criminal was quoted as saying:

"Are you sure it's safe?"

A strange and ironic final question from a man who was about to be put to death for the ghastly crimes that he had committed.

Printed in Great Britain
by Amazon